REPORT PLANET

BOOK BY PHILIP KIDD AND AUTOBIOGRAPHY

PHILIP KIDD

BALBOA.PRESS
A DIVISION OF HAY HOUSE

Balboa Press books may be ordered through booksellers or by contacting:

Balboa Press
A Division of Hay House
1663 Liberty Drive
Bloomington, IN 47403
www.balboapress.com.au
AU TFN: 1 800 844 925 (Toll Free inside Australia)
AU Local: 0283 107 086 (+61 2 8310 7086 from outside Australia)

ISBN: 978-1-5043-2496-0 (sc)
ISBN: 978-1-5043-2495-3 (e)

Print information available on the last page.

Balboa Press rev. date: 03/25/2021

INTRODUCTION

INCOME RECIEPTED
4 020 000 000 000
MONIES STOLEN > 10 .2 B PROFFIT 8470
3 972 000 000 000 2012-2018
AFRICA BORDERS 80 000 000 PA HOBBY PURPOSE 120 B PA
NETT 1 596 856 725
AUS BUSINESS COMPONENT ROI 511M + 23 550 000
HOUSEHOLD INCOME
242 000 PA
england account 22 000 000

we have jurisdiction in 240 39 191 countries we respond to written searches the search fee made in cheque in AUD from the Institue Office Lively records. There is a REPORT in each Nation in each Year. All our works is done in the WORLD COMPUTER in Which we have built since 1976 since 1982. Found in 1980 of importance is our assets which benefit each person in the world now 8 000 000 000 and service animals. In our time Global Warming Content is reduced by 50% and we contribute to the Maintainance of Global Warming Reductions.

We are also one of the worlds leading nuclear experts. We work for each Nation and Union of Nations how we achieve to make a benefit for all people in the world and our primary offices span the planet and we can get work done. We are continually building. Philip is a Successful Commercial-writer and has run the 6 biggest developments for the world. The people whom do the work of developments are in alignment called celestial. We aligned with Elizabeth Hilton the people whom in alignment are the developer called celeste and together we are the worlds biggest builder. Philip kidd space and the people are an individual entity. Our other corums are staff devoted to citicens experience.

The world has 6 improvement in the 2nd generation and a better world and have achieved the same countries borders. less have died and people live longer. Lalaine and Philip are region and region. Philip is Rocketman and was the former region technical rocketmen. Berlin and Philip own the 10 Barristers which each service person has travelled in in majatron the 1st side of the world or rocketman the 2nd side of the world. Lalaine has the most success entity born in 15 generations 100% of the Ally 3 is made it home. The world has seen the greatest achievments in the history of the world and people have more babies. The world population explosion is a result of success and is to be embraced not feared.

The worlds first work is security just like for thousands of years. The worlds 2nd work because of success is to feed 20 billion people work is already underway we always have plenty to do. The work of the world is run and done in writing and serves each person one day to be 20 000 000 000 people the global family. The articulation is done inside a computer. By 2019 after 35 years of building the world is run by giant computers. Philip worked to supply home from 1980-2000 and we had a successful home we earnt 28 000 000 and our organisations were paid 940 000

000 AUD which we invested in our organisations. We have met the worlds demand and I have grown double the number of staff in each world calendar.

If you work from the report your nation has not obscured secret the same as we do and as we do the work for each nation and race. we work for 27 000 races. lalaine and Philip earned

2 800 000 from engagements. We made it in 2020 we have done allright lalaine is a beautifull partner. I am a good husband as lalaine expresses our time. We had an affluent life . we have had a large amount of monies stolen each and every transit, we now live a luxury life and lalaine supports our family for a retirement whom is middle class. We have 5

properties to live in and for office and a weekender. 3

are beachouses and we have had a life by the sea and good friends. lalaine has paid and paid for 4 years. our organisations are paid to 2024.

we are paid to 2022. lucis is paid. the rule is paid. the citicens are paid for the nation wall. Writing is complete at governor of NSW 2015. Our organisations have 494 properties in total and STORE

DOWNLOAD MY FULL RESUME C.V.
RESUME PUBLICATIONS Life Story 2
New Page

2022 REPORT

IT IS A PLEASURE TO BE IN CHARGE IN THE YEARS WITH THE BEST
RESULTS AND BIGGEST RESULT IN THE WORLD AND THE HIGHEST
ACHIEVEMENT. THE PEOPLE IN CHARGE IN THE TIME OF AUNTY LEONIE
AUNTY JANET HAD
THE BEST EVER RESULTS IN THE WORLD AND THE BEST WEAPONS RESULTS.35.
OUR Business Organisations and Institutions Are Built and Get Income From THE NATIONS
IN THE WORLD ETHIC and We Serve ALIGNED NATIONS.
I am a leading Boss of Aligned Nations A Boss of the World and We Got 3 Owners $1, 596, 856, 725 AUD Distributable currency. Our organisation is run in the work the world computers.
we keep income and expenditure and staff logs and do reciept and build report i keep the books for each organisation
and the service of the kingdom of aisles. we have 494 properties.
940, 000, 000 AUD RECIEPT Was invested in INVESTMENT II. and we have engaged
DOUBLE THE NUMBER OF STAFF meeting the
Worlds Population growth. Stipends are Paid. Taxations in

Each country are Paid. In the australian business component is the operating monies for AUS is
Account england 22 000 000

CHEQUE   >22 500 000 DISORDERED INTERNAL ACTION

APPARTMENT BAYSWATER 750 000 Settlement monies stolen from bank account

70 000 deposit paid to builder, reciept

INVESTIGATION AND ACTIONS BY REGION

1998   5600 Disturbed and monies stolen

charges laid by human courts 17 years in a row o respondent

Building by party international investigation

2000   75 000 PAY OUT

1980-2000   28 000 000 MADE   philip cinamen

2000-2020   23 550 000 RAISED philip lalaine

438 000 invested 65-72 philip lalaine

REPAIR   34 000 000 STOLEN

34 000 000 PAID SETTLED MONIES MISSING IN PASSAGE

MARCH 2013   STAFF WAGES NOT PAID MONIES NOT SETTLED

FULL AMBIENT INVESTIGATION

END OF 2013 INVESTIGATORS 1500 PUT ON

2012   SETTLEMENT OF NEW ECONOMIES AUSTRALIA DAY

PHILIP INDICE 48

LIEGH 39

2013   FULL ARMERY

WORLDS BIGGEST ACHIEVEMENT

REGION STRATA REPAIR 34 000 000 MONIES MISSING IN TRANSIT

2015 $511 000 000 AUD CURRENCY ROI 420 000 000 WAGES HELD

Birth Family   23 farms 26 000 000 000 banking. Drought 2019

commerce board

BORDERS COST 4 000 000 000

4 000 000 000

fees   6 600 000

continued fees 6 000 000

distribution   4 500 000

OFFICE COST 19 500 000

England,   2,200 000 000 RULE PAID

2 200 000 000 debtor creditors 2000

creditors 2000 2020

donation 9% paid interest 31 000, 3 500

1974   156 000 actions by nations

Yacht racing, museum effects

INCOME/EXPENDITURE

open 2000 475 000
INCOME 28 000 000
EXPENDITURE 28 000 000
CASH 400 000, 200 000
      750 000
           1 800 000 maintainance
TERRACE 10 000 000
balance 2010 1 000 000

open 2010 1 000 000
2007 250 000 working
           1 500 000 maintainance
INCOME 23 550 000
EXPENDITURE 19 500 000
COST OF OFFICE 19 500 000
LALAINE INCOME 0.261M PHP
LALAINE EXPENSES PHP 0.261M
commerce board,15 generations
2017 250 000 working
Balance Family 86 000
      101 000 000
open 2020 101 000 000

_____donation 9% Paid_____

DISTRIBUTED 1 MAY 2020 $182 000 AUD personal taxation to be settled
balance of personal account   1990-2000 240 000PA
        2000-2010   353 000PA
        2010-2020   740 000PA
        HOUSEHOLD INCOME 2014-2022 $242 000PA
        fbt=680 000

COST = 0
cost = 0
cost to friends = 0
friends paid cost of work
Credit 0   0   1.7%   1.29%   0   0   14000
\   COST = > 220 000 000 000
COST = 460 000 paid by friends

COST = 140 000 written off 2019 philip lalaine

friends paid 1.93M

Friends assembled against, international hearings, inquest

human courts findings

no berthright by christians

COST = 200 000

156 000 COUNCELLED TWICE

COST 2020 = 0

\ Travel 4500 lalaine HOME Antipolo 400PM fees 300PM

BW 8000 8500

Medical costs 16 000

\

SOURCES   Philip funders

New Owners

Bankking 360 000 000 000 hk1

Balance business = 0   PAID TO 2024

Balance   = 167 000 overseas.

250 000 working

65-72 643 000

PAID TO 2022

REQUIRED   1600PW

1 600 000 Maintainance

PAY OUT CREDITORS

FINALISE DISTRIBUTION

ARRANGE IN PLACE OF DICTATE

PAY FOR REGION EXCURSIONS @ REGION STAFF CONDEMNED

AND DISPERSED 20.11.2013, 2 staff in street.

PAY LAY AT United Nations New Generation Office BANGKOK.

PAY FOR WRITTEN COMMUNICATION REGION TRAVELS CUT

FINALISE WALL PATTAYA CONFERENCE CENTRE.

ARCHIVE PHOTOGRAPHS, DOCUMENTS

CONCEEDURE TO PAY FOR STORE.

INVESTIGATION OUTCOME and RESULT

INQUEST OUTCOME and RESULT

Identity = Commoner

RECORDS = HUMAN COURTS RECORDS
INTERNATIONAL COURTS SETTLEMENTS
MONIES TO BE IDENTIFIED
Fuel Berths - Siphon, OBSCURE, Newcastle Pipeline.
GERTH 1974
Praises NSW Kogorah St george hospital, medicare hernia
  " " " " " " Infection, Antibiotics Injection.
  " " " " " " " Infection, Antibiotics IV.
DR Tony Mazaferro DR Daniel Llambi. Lucis cleaning and attendence
REGION RECORDS TAYLOR SQUARE REGION STAFF SICK
LEAVE PRICE WATERHOUSE STAFF England not Paid, Ordered
to be on REGION SALARY.
PUMP DIESEL AMERICA SHIPS SUPER TANKER
THE REGION CAN NOW REFUELL A C5
SHIPPING LANES 2 MATERS SHIPPING RECORDS HONG
KONG. OFFICE HONG KONG
IMMUNION 9
ASIA PACIFIC REGION HEAD OFFICE JAPAN. CONGRESS
PLAIN PNG
INTERNAL SECRETARY-GENERAL, SECRET SERVICE.
PRESIDENTS CALL-TAIWAN.
PORT REGION 1

I WAS INSTRUCTED TO BUILD ASSETTS REGISTER 2018
Our assetts are already recorded and laid.
Access is destroyed.
Our capacity for england is destroyed. The Identity is the same, equal
Identity.
FINAL TRIAL 2019 Philip has cleared / Passed 1,116 trials formed
from the record laid. The staff have cleard trial and takes vengence, I
get Help With staff security.
In the Past i did all the work myself. in 2020 lalaine and i have 75% of
the things we used to do . 46 hours a week. Was 110 hours a week. I
WAS APPOINTED AND INSTALLED TO DO THE WEAPONS
WORK 2015
FOR THE NATIONS OF THE WORLD. MY STAFF WILL DO
THE WORK,
I HAVE BUILT THE SUPPLY. I WILL EARN 4,000,000,000,000
IN THE ERA. WE WILL BE DOWN 190 BILLION DOLLARS

D.TRUMP 2017 and Sales England and have paid for additional passage 30,000,000,000.

THE WORK REFUSED TO WORK WITH CITICENS OF England and I put in

400 000 hours of work but i couldnt get a result. By 2020

There is adjustment, also we have now no job under 3B,

IF WE ARE SHORT OF MONEY WE WILL NOT COMPLETE NATIONS PAYMENTS

TO WEAPONS MANUFACTURERS for PRODUCT INTERNAL. WE WILL FORTIFY RECIEPT INSTEAD OF ISSUING RECIEPT. MY NEW OWNERS MIGHT APPLY TO MY FUNDERS FOR

UP TP 150 000 000 000 AT THE MOST AND AT THIS TIME WE CANT SPEND OUR BANKING. WE NEED TO BANK MORE THAN 3.5%. LALAINE HAS COMPLETED BOOKS> OUR ASSETTS ARE INTACT IN 2020. WE MADE IT IN 2020. THE WORLD HAS HAS WORKED MANY MANY YEARS TOWARDS 2020, THE WORLDS BIGGEST PLANS SINCE END BC Jesus0 0AD RECOVERY and PASSAGES, I WAS INTRODUCED TO THE PLANS IN 1980. AT THIS TIME WE HAVE PENTY OF MONEY. IN 2015 PLENTY OF MONEY, ENOUGH MONEY, IN 2010 PLENTY OF MONEY, ENOUGH MONEY. PHILIP after

23 years in yacht racing finished yacht racing. Philip Played golf for 38 years. we went on many dancefloors. i did body surf and i have been on every beach from adelade to brisbane and flew over the great australian bight in my time off in engagements. Philip and lalaine in engagements and appointments have travelled half way around asia. we have been to 240 destinations and had dinner. at 59 my arteries are clean inside and full blood flow from a balanced meal each meal. i have lived an active life more than most people do and i worn

out my joints, old age at 52. my body has done a lot of work and climbing and many miles on foot. in asia we did 120 000 km and 200 km week on foot and lalaines legs wore out.

i did 1 400 000 km in australia 50% in my private car GT. All the work was done to make the writing sucessfull and from 1980-2000 to SUPPLY home my 2nd Career.

The writing is sucessful and I am a Sucessful Commercial-Writer. We have Signed, sealed and deliverd a whole planet now 8 000 000 000 People.

I ran the worlds 6 biggest developements and ran up the new triens. My Grand father father was ward the seat of india and ran the developement of australia and surrounds. My great grandfather was the first ward. In 1991 i was installed and i and my staff ran the developements of australia and surrounds all the way to statements. after the event

I handed over the ward which are the people seat of india canada australia south africa 6 countries to HRH after the event. We had in the 4-6 most results in the world, my staff did and impeccable job and my 22 000 volunteers in ward 4. I built the nuclear retail supply and passages to 70 countries and handed over to the new generation in 2014 the kingdom made fortunes and i was paid handsomely. England rely to the nations is england got rich from coal thresa may for the protestant and rich 2019. we are pleased to see adani up, up. It is very healthy to supply india. india has design nuclear reactors and in 15 years it is likey for general electric to build a line of nuclear reactors. We know the busines well, my staff ELECTRIC LABORITORY ROZELLE DIVISION ARE NUCLEAR EXPERTS AND DO WORK FOR EVERY COUNTRY IN THE WORLD. WE HAVE MADE GOOD DECISIONS. I HAVE ALL THE NUCLEAR LICENCES, I HAVE ALL THE DEVELOPEMNET LICENCES. THE STAFF OF PHILIP KIDD - SPACE ARE EXEPTIONALLY QUALIFIED AND ARE WORLD LEADING EXPERT. WE HAVE DONE SPACE SINCE 1976 and Dignity,

MY FIRST CAREER. I HAVE BUILT AND DONE THE WORK WITH MY FRIENDS AND THE DEEDS ARE OWNED BY CINAMEN, PHILIP AND LALAINE

IN 2019 2020 WE ARE 1,300,000 PEOPLE. We are Awarded. These are the works in australia i have been paid for in the 20 years. For autralia internal i built the 4B transmission works.

We did a secondary work to raise monies to supply the autralian business component because monies were stolen we raised 23 550 000 more than most people can raise gave us enought money to maintain our assetts luckily. my partners are beutifull and immaculate

and for all the years i have been called lucky phil. In the years
I am called the cowboy, and the People staff whom do the work for Your country is philip and lalaine 460 000 staff the cowboy space Legacy. I am Doctor, I am also a member, citicen.

I am Employer, Partner, family member.

In 1980 I am the one whom directed the work to be done and have kept all the way. In 2015 I retired and by 2020 all the work i have directed to be done is done and i am finished by 2020. Each business is in Proffit and is run from BP'99 BP2000 by our new owners and our organisation is fully serviced. from 1982 we have grown from a donation by berlin porsche my business partner to a

4,000,000,000,000 empire. We have always been people people and our hallmark is we love people. I am glad to be a good boss. I have been boss 50% of the time since

1988.

MY GERTH IN England was A high school Prefect, voted. My later Gerth ids defender. I am a member of the world defender and an underwriter. our business pays for our activity as a dignity. Philip and Lalaine

are Region, Region, I am ROCKETMAN from 2000. I have funders. Lalaine is a dignity, commerce board and born in 15 generations. Philip is head of secret service. I started, pool salesman. Lalaine is Boss, Philip is boss of the world since 1996. All my people are retired now and my people are a new generation.

In my lifetime i have met each person born to it the 3 500.

I have also done each signature and kept each record.

There are Diplomatic Embassies. Our lobby s keep record of Diplomatic consorts and have on diplay the diplomatic embassies made nation to nation. The Kingdom of Aisles Valley Nunn at Our Emerald Palace MAKE the dignities from nations giving hospice at our palace to the dignities and making the FORMAL RECORD. The records we have are distributed to each nation in the world and union of nations. In each year we build a report. Now I am Retired this is the lasting report. ALL OUR WORK IS ON DVD.

ALL MY WORK IS IN SAFES. ALL OUR WORK FOR England is ON VIDEO LIBRARY. IF you are enmbamed you haveeverlasting life 3000 years later and the mummies are still on. Our work on library is such good quality we expect you will Live longer.

COPYWRIGHT HOUSE OF COCONUT AND WOOD 2020.
OFFICE HONG KONG
Antipolo.
1980-2020
REGISTER. ANSTERDAM.
KOREA. ELECTRIC LABORITORY.
The rocket science factory korea i s now the largest institution in the world now serving over 5 600 000 people will include you. I am a member of institutions. I for many years am board member of ramada and astoria are most favoured and Staffer for
philips corporation, and we are partner General electric and
have the plans for each model power station. I have won a lot

in yacht racing and went aboard wild oats IV the maxi the 4 time line winner of the sydney to hobart yacht race. My staff and i
have long term done the space and switching for yacht races all over the world.it is our exclusive hobby.
In english retired scientist. I watched every canterbury game for 30 years while it was televised and didnt miss one game. OUR HALL IS FINISHED AT CANTERBURY, DISPLAY HURLSTONE PARK. WE WILL SEE YOU AT THE ANMM PYRMONT. From the newly built equipment you have done many rescues and with the new equipment and drones donated by america you have in the region saved many lives.
We have got the big results together. we are substantial rulers, We saved the power station we are the legends of rescue and
we are the priority emergency attendent in the world. Nowadays space workers work from the new suburb in space.
The legend swings from thomas the tank in manila park a real tangible and the datum in our world is run from the pyramids, egypt. OFFICE EGYPT
LAID BY GEOFFRY ROBERTSON.
PHILIP KIDD
ELIZABETH HILTON
MEDIAN OFFICE CHINA HERITAGE PALACE SUPPLY
PRINCESS CHINA, DOMAIN.
THE ORIGINAL BUILT IS WITH Uncle.
I HAVE JURASDICTION IN 240 39 191 Counties.
My new built office spans the world and reaches right throughout the universe and my chair 2001 reaches, built over 15 years, THANK YOU. In the worlds time the building flew in space registered one of the worlds most competent designs and saved the day.
EMBARGO. HUMMERS.
MANUSCRIPT Telephone apple iphone
MANIPULATION NONE
Our hummers have full armery which means the aerial can reach right through the world rightinto the planet and right into and
through the universe and do space and dialect from the design plans laid on
the table in our hummers from inside the hummer more than my office can do even though my office has the longest span. we will keep it running as long as we run our hummers.
Live corporate has 35 000 clients the 35 000 rule of the world.
WE Can duplicte our contact with 35000 rule in the world and you have range

with 35000 rule in the world part of your sucess. We congratulate
your sucess and the inherent world population growth.we are both
sucessful. I thank roy and HG for doing the deeds for me . the work for
you was done by tim flannery you call the walking encylepedia.
you can look up the past on wikepedia. PHILIP HAS AUTHOUR
WITH PEACE.
WHITE ARE MYSELF IN PERSON IN OUR WORLD AND SIGN
FOR ME.
I have done pathways all my life and i have done billions of passages. It
is from my grandfather whom did PATHWAYS
and in daytime was accountant. My grandfather on the fathers side was
an astronomer whom made discovery and
Ward, England Seat of India, in daytime was Accountant. My mother
and father met on the train and kept up, lived around the corner from
each other, the history is written up and the figures information and
history is in each
part of the world and laid are the results. My father
was Developer like his father and grandfather and so was uncle ted
kidd, Was Ward, England Seat of India, Grandmaster thence strength
freemasons and lead for many years,
in daytime was partner plumber business thence senior prosecutor to
53. each lived an old age.
My mother was Theologian. Ma was affluent. Grandma was
Housewife. In all the years housewife is the highest post it might be
different
for you today but not in most of the world. This is particulary
what the housewife wanted. in all our family the was no violence and
no amount of violence and also for me and cinamen and is freedom the
housewife the grand wanted. I can tell you the
women were grand women. The great granfather and grandmother
owned a farm
and then built a huge business a blacksmith workshop and had a lot
of money to raise 11 children. there are many children in the family.
The granparents had business and were in charge of business and
built the foundation for parramatta, today parramatta is a modern
city, in the spare time built the parramatta bowling club, grandfather
was chairman. in each year i go there myself lived and buried in
parramatta the children retired in parramatta and yes believe it drove
a kingswood. the father and mother opened the first chain stores in
australia, stock agents in thier daytime. in then the land in burwood
was expensive and i f you could afford the land you build your mansion
in burwood and so how times have changed now a mansion is built to

the waterfront. brighton 200 years ago had 120000 people of a 200000 poulation to the beach on steamtrian and tram. brighton today still has 100-200000 people to the beach but the populationis 24 000 000. the children parents lived in burwood and each relation and in the wheat belt. The farms as annette was shown the farms had 1 billion dollar crop each. the family today are still on the farms and by ratio there is 276 children. my family is in sydney 2000 and then my family is in the philippines whom are born and middle class.

Each had a beautifull home or mansion -Homestead and drove a holden one had a dodge phoenix and one had a rolls royce. The friends were Rich and thier help or contribution meant all the work was done and done on time as we were taught to.

Mum was a member and officer of country womens association. We met on the telephone at 6 and built with the people born overseas. in my time i have met each person born in the 3500

The work is done from writing and the people have built writing. It was indivisible in the event which defense was possible the ones whom didnt do written, we followed up for the ones whom didnt do written by instructing a conveyance and got results. We have instructed the response.

The costs in the world and to each country have been extravagent as we can see in hindsight 7 years after the cost of addressing offender. As is my job I have wriiten it up. There are good results.

I have lived my 1ST Career and we have been awarded. I have been Boss for many years and appreciate the results.

My mother born built a fund for me in 1966 and a fund for Annette. Annette was put in charge. The Descendency is with the females. Annette has special memories like Paster IIX whom of mt riverview church had 8 mistresses at his wife. The son was dunked in his swimming pool and he got a bung.

All this started when the nations wouldnt marry henry IIX to his 8th Wife. This is not the first time the race has been rejected. Response will get thr race out of it. At this time there is no Closed weapons on IRAQ, INDONESIA. WW3 hangs in the balance.

The race won inhabitation occupation against the ascension the biggest won in the world but it is not repaired. Can you predict what strength will call the shots paster or commoner. Can you build a charting. the birth family are modellers from chartings the birth family in generations traditionally built modells to service the world, i have the history of 380 years. In GENESIS the first book of the BOUND you can see the Affluent Modell The world of the time was run from. Each world leader filled in thier raceNations details in the

BERTH as the Peoples of God, Kings of Kings Gave the world leaders hospice in thier land, for over 15 5000 years.

The most famous Berth is solomon Israel Judah, Sheba Ethiopia. Solomon and sheba Fell in love in the hospitalice in thier quarters and after continued to see each other, Solomon and sheba got married and made and brought the two kingdoms together. Who will be the next and whom will be the most number of citicens. the worlds mission to defend citicens is sucessfull.

I was first taught in sunday school, the secret is in the songs. For the first time in 3500 years the world has experienced a times of no war between countries the original aim. Can you Project.

The balance of nations is innocent. australia and surrounds input is anzac day commemorative.a prediction in the mass of people. the lower case stay in the mass by salute and are not in the masses. Thus we can present a larger number. Our Voice. The missions are peacetime missions.

Of the mass or consequence you need a degree to understand it. I was confirmed. We have been in the business 42 years. I have paid 40 years. When we were 16 our first clients were elizabeth II and philip, determined to make the world a better place. we have each contributed to making the world a better place. I built my empire once entreprenur then empire then fluent from a donation by a ruler 16 years old from her 360 billion dollars inheritence. hays was paid 360 billion dollars for his work payment called inheritence, philip and hays are the youngest in the business. we all started in 22 years of age, our first instructions were to recover the gulf war, we didnt know what to do, it is a different story since the people have brought you the best results and we thank each one. Hays was my best mate when I was 20, I installed Hays. For the communities Matthew has done the work. Matthew got the work right.

Elizabeth Hilton born the developer celeste and i and my people the developer celestial aligned and today we are the worlds biggest builder. I built the 120 nations solidarity long mental health board and we were awarded it works effectively.

All our thank yous, awards are laid at taiwan so our people which come from every nation can see thier awards. My record as a boss of the world is at ireland hall.

I did appointments with Kerry my second.

I had dinner saturday night. Cinamen and I met with friends and went out.

and i would call in to see my mother in law and brother. I was on the telephone reguarly with my father in law,

My father in law died at a young age of a heart attack.

We wanted more time together and completed to end up in another plan. We had 20 good years all in sydney 2000. cinamen never left the city. I went all over australia. after i went overseas. we did the biggest signature at engagement which was overseas. on the following day we went to stay at location and saw 1000 black chinese limousines in manila.

it is beyond the capacity of former generations for the peoples of our world to achieve so much and so much love.we saw france at manila on our television in TV produce. what we saw was the same as the plans. each mission today is peace missions. My writing is in terrain. I did my 1st work at 14.

With the members of INSTITUTE I and we build the long world table proceedure the reconcilliation tables with your work the new world. I was in charge of running up the new generation triens. George bush with hope talked many times about the new world and now the new world is built and serves every person.

We have signed sealed and delivered a whole planet and the records for the future is laid and also your record laid on the floors of one love. our love and tribute to the global family we have spent our life with. wayne swan, boss did the deeds for england. when it came to giving testimony annette didnt know any of this, is all the paperwork missing we have billions of dollars to work from annette had $o. the most number of dead is acts of god, the sucess is you are attending, thence the murders and damage, thence corona virus,

there is no war between countries, war in countries you have troops in place, your are flooding sucessfully.

the space work is run from the new suburb in space

the world is run sucessfully, the 3 are in writing 2017.

SEAL IS MADE AT THE GOVERNOR OF NSW 2015. Yhe race has not the most secure ethic but it is good, the 27000 races each race has secure ethic. more to come when you make it into the future. we hope you

are comfortable aboard. At the END you Are CLEAR. we have found there isnt room for an aggressor. The UN CHIEF B BEAZELY has given the figures / statistics ARCHIVE NineMsn. Wikepedia, British empire

Wikepedia Post Office

WEAPONS UNION 35% HISTORY IMMACULATE TO 2013 14 years 0 = DEAD PRESENT HISTORY ASCENSION 2013 START 2009 Past history 1999 2006

LAST NUMBER OF DEAD 1968 Your history 1St record 1996

Germany = 0 = Innocent Holland innocent Ireland innocent
what happened to israel wont happen again but the central region has
had the highest problems. Our people are on the
2nd side of the world as region region the majority of our
people are bhuddist, we own CAMP with china and have manned
CAMP we had
750 000 people through camp Turkey sapphire and there are 250 000
people in camp North Borders turkey sapphire. over 1 100 000 people
have a new country, you have excelled. Christians gave/handed
out water. You supply 1500 diesels. This is not the end of your story.
This is your story to our time. we are finished. Philip has recorded
since 1996 now for 8 000 000 000 the strength of sucess.
Your new generation bosses will write your story up from here. Philip
remained a boss.

WE ARE RETIRED IN 2020, All my people have retired. my people
are a new generation. in join we have 1.3 million people and staff, We
live out our days, friends, BOSS BOSS, member, founder,
commerce board 15 generations, Region, Region ASIA-PACIFIC
REGION, CITICEN
INVESTOR, Lalaine OWN. Philip is EON, Lalaine is millionair but
the monies we can draw from is minus. there are 1500 investigtors
put on.
3 for each country, I have jurasdiction in 240 39 191 Countries.
I have done extensive work for the british empire and we were paid
handsomely. For my empire i have funders. At the end of a lifetime of
study, we have all the offices and we give the longest education
in the world. each business is in proffit.
We have all the developements Licences, I have all the space Licences
and I have all nuclear licence and a diploma in energy systems.
I am a bacheor of arms warrant and writt, Alignment doctor.
In my 2nd career was corporate of a 1.8 billion dollar company and paid
for home, an exclusive home and support and the attention voluntary
works.
Lalaine is affluent, excecutive, Investor, Awards, specialist and career
paid for home. lalaine brought a nice home.
I live out my days Senior Assasin, HEAD, EMPLOYER, PARTNER,
family member.
and we look forward to the years. we have our people in place. we
support 5-6 people.
as boss it was my obligation to have expert in place. some of

the expert in place are my staff, our staff are awarded and also awarded
3 times in a row for saving the most number of
lives in the world and we hugely
appreciate the help we have had. at the end of the worlds big
developement
there are 5 presidents in a row. all is on dvd . the worlds
information is on dvd. in each national broadcaster the information is
individual in 4400 languages and image. We thank SONY SCREENS
Whom have been there in person. all my work is in
safes. An ABC Respondent has been there for me on behalf of the
number of the worlds population at the privelage of the Authour seaL.
all my work for the british isles and british people
is on video library. The worlds work is in 3900 languages. The work of
my organisations is done in the worlds computers. I am a member. It
has been a pleasure to know you.
Our organisation now is fully serviced. White sign for me. We notice
you have given up fighting wars on horseback but our names come
from the old days, we dont have children,
yah=hoo signs off and gives over to yeh-hah, aunty leonie has
descendents. The cowgirl is at the top of the tree are the CHART. You
have done many works which are sucessfull and is known
as the worlds plans. your service has got medals and we apply a thank
you. as i am citicen australia and surrounds
Tom uren and Angus heuston got the highest awards.
Tom lead and was in charge of the reconcilliation of the indigeonous,
angus was her majesty quarter. Our region is
our house in the middle of our street and our love is a light. We have
worked together with the citicens of the kingdoms.
we are nearly one third of the worlds population.
When you engaged me there were many staff and service and the
worlds work is 0.5 billion people, now i have retired we are 1 300 000
people when we are engaged. I am boss of
100%. the peoples in 27000 constitutions, the united nations the
peoples in 26000 constitutions over 86% of the worlds populations
and the united nations represent thier members.
I long done the worlds work and do the work for all, our organisations
are private entities and we do work for 27000
races. our clients are 35000 rules of the 45000 rules in the world we
help make it better for thier citicens. The money I earn pays
for both work in the world. as was the founding plan all the work done
is to make the writing sucessfull. leading my education was
philip button and pearl button. For england My bosses were Wrath and

Bath

and my mentor was dawn chambers. In work for the world Philip, greece was my

first ever boss. Philip built all of our registries. I built my Office in Hong Kong and we began building. We have surveyed billions of staff we worked hard, each member has made a contribution to the world which has increased benefit to each citicens and made the worlds a vastly better place. The results of work I have written up is some of the testaments and form part of the worlds testables

we are to lay at United Nations, New Generation Office BANGKOK. When I was 20 I had a group of people whom wanted to help me

in the work i was born to, and began work and I have had sucess ever since, these gracefull men were still doing work after 30 years.

It is true good decisions have got us there but it is the help we have had by which we have made it. I wish you continued sucess. The purpose of work is security as is for thousands of years,

the 2nd purpose new on the horizon

is to feed 20 billion people. so far transit is built throughout the world the supply shipping containers. start in 1980 solomon

lieu coles transit is built. Reticulation will have to be built we are on the way. Philip is a Governor of Crisis the worlds Newest continent, we built the new suburb in space, the citicens built the vegetable garden in space. philip is the developer in bangladesh the worlds latest developement the gift of the people of thailand to thier nieghbour. we are doing inspections.

The goverance of south america continent is installed. Agreements Documents and Records laid by members commerce board philippines. I know as 15 generations.

many years ago, My ancestors moved from the kingdom of aisles to europe shore to build, more than 350 years ago

my ancestors moved from europe the the other side

of the world to build the second side of the world we live in today. the second side of the world is built.

In australia the anscestors set up an income for 180 years.

The Valley nunn are on tour and the Valley nunn have been in charge. Today is anzac day and is interupted by the corona virus, at 6am this morning the bugle sounded the last ode in our street.

the commemorative is at the memorial on soil in our street and a candle is lit. it took everyone in the world to make

the world a better place. The plan of writing is everyone has

a contribution. we wish you peace in your suburb. also you can make a huge difference in the world by being good in your suburb. Australia

has the worlds first womens mates club, 3 nsw parlainment women
mocking the fable mates club, the girls have done the negotiations,
the girls relied they have completed by writing the cheques, but I
did the numbers, the girls song is on abc news 24,
the girls havent written the cheques the most important conduct of a
politician. It has all started again, will our suburb crash.
the bhuddist world made
perfect conduct, the thai cave rescue didnt go above the mayor. It is
the nicest and lovely to be so proficient. Ive finished the report, called
its a long way to tipperary, the books are done are called lalaine is a
millionaire. my uncle bob came back from the frontline of 2 world
wars.
It is great outcomes to be a good arms surveyor and a sucessfull
assasin. we hosted in each Nation. one commercial-writer was shot. the
apply of
good writing has made the world a better place. It is also very
generous lalaine to be a sucessfull investor.

IT IS GREAT FORTUNE TO BE A SUCESSFUL Commercial-
Writer. If you want something special you can see the wisdom wall
chinese gardens ermita manila.

ARCHIVE 2020

MADE IT IN 2020
1980-2020
18-2020 my writing is in terrain, near china, avenues high the palaces and world table and reaches
above eaves, below kinngdom.
we got the money in beachouse. we have/are retired 2020. I still own a business, we own a
business. I retired from all
the other things we do and lalaine has retired and retired from hairdressing lalaine gets
740pw 270pw notes, was born
and gets the balance of monies. there is distribution . the grandparents were commercial rice
farmers and 88.
my 2 new owners and my study and study in the philippines and head of staff laywers and
accountants

instruction run the conduct and the business fully serviced.white run the empire. to do work from report does supply

secret and 0 damage. we made a report each year and is distributed to the nations. there are few dealings with people whom chop rights.

we have served many people and we have supplied company secret.

my staff ran the recovery, the people of a business. my staff built a nuclear relay. at the end of my studies i have all nuclear licences, i have all developement licence . for the nations there is an expert in place. our work id is done in the world computers. from 1982 i built the office hong kong. lalaine continues investor.

Philip lalaine duties employer partner citicen member home2, weekender

11 properties 6 properties to live in and office, 1 sold, 10 properties 5 properties to live in and office. 494 properties, 493 properties. Assetts assets.

pictorial platens photographs precious embassies records, past we have nations records, past missionary, pictorial to nations.awards philip and lalaine is region, region philip is rocketman head of secret service governor of crisis developer in bangladesh a gift from nieghbour thailand anmm project 3d vision nation and anglican church

Lutheran landlord 10.000 share vincent is demonstrator \vince share meg

at the top paul, priority and priority people staff commiserate for nations bobb carr seat john kerry, kerry 2 philip 2second for the world secretay sandra

for the region region laywer roslyn, retired

for the kingdoms bosses principle valley nunn, stay emerald palace above reaches on border the bosses of england flew to russia and did sign the surrender. we sign the defense at novatel.

the work is done the citicens have immunion, we have a second immunity. philip and lalaine. lucis has a mature and made claim 40 000. lucis is paid. region 1 grant

for the born orina birth . line rosalina. for the born grant doel. signature and

constellation annette doel. i am related. there was harm in the bloodlines, there is work done in the bloodlines i wasnt related.in the 2nd generation

we are the 2nd generation of our world petra. our board is galactic sta harmonica.

our boards are function.intercontinental daybreaker phoenix harmony, firestones, platypus the borders in africa continent are being built. my staff are in charge of building

borders africa continent and we are paid 80 000 000 000pa and there is good progress. the rule is paid. we have maintained our assetts. the assetts of the internal organisation was distributed lalaine and philip made a proffit of 8470 from the entire empire.

ASSETTS MAINTAINED

IN THE 2ND ERA ASSETTS MAINTAINED

WORK ON ASSETTS DONE

2020 Philip and Lalaine

ASSETTS TO BE RUNNING

TAXATIONS AUSTRALIA TO BE SETTLED

LAID TO BANGKOK

INVESTIGATORS 1500 2013
beginning 2013
PAID 2018

CHARLES MASSIH = Pay off your home loan. the purpose is to lock in the loan repayment
amount the savings achieved and have a property consumed we can live in have office and
store of
6 properties to live in and office. the two property achieve the required space. we can migrate
from port maquarie to old bar as i would have migrate
from bayswater to wolli creek owner office. rent paid 2001 - 2020. office disbanded, office in
place. the owners
office ran 16 years. office of dignity office expert in place, the residence is not settled we were
overseas and have not made it back.chargeable costs. fbt = 680 000
2020 fbt = 56 000 the obligations and commitments were met 81 000 pa
HOUSEHOLD INCOME 2014-2022 $242 000 PA philip lalaine lucis.
man shawn. for 180 000 000 000 8 000 000 000 claim occupation inhabitation was awarded and
arms set. assylum built for syrria
philip has cv resume records awards 1980-2020 lalaine has cv records. response awards
genesis was lifted the 156000 was not settled.

750 000
156 000
international courts settlements

for the working party royalties some royalties were settled
30 000 - 45 000 valued at inflation 2.5 times work 1.0 2.0 i earned double all the way, chart.
2012 credit = 0
the citicens are paid.
the citicens did 0 searches. the nations did 0 searches. darwin treaty should be full function.
to recover start from darwin treaty see what function exist. recover taxation computres. plan
genesis is function. the work is perfect. the calculation is stored.
JFK
afterweapons built and constructed usa porting out of hawaii. wrong direction supply 12 ships
going good
armed forces in right supply 2015
right 2015
right at the centre of chambers {centre of computer} 2015
if the taxation computers are recovered we will get o monies back there will be a co-latereal
supply at the imputs deformed, disordered.
if each execution warrant is produced we will get 0 monies back the will be o person counted.
where settled dna dentures. otherwise there is an irrelevent output all computers in a linear equal
to survey - tripgeographical.

work is finished volumes are finished. 7 years
SENSE
the weapons done are 18%
the response is 86% 0f the worlds population.
the high weapons are stable the ground weapons are problem

function in assetts on 205 000
the empire was run from 4 of 39 accounts and supply dignity. there is 0 repentence yet. there
were 0 other monies and 0 compensation and 0 settled CLAIM. the parents claim is for costs of
evacuation. the calculation and computers input = 0
thus 0 in 1/0
SENSE

THIS IS THE END OF TESTABLES
1ST MAY 2020.
Easter 16 th April 2020
TESTAMENT Made it christmas 2019 and
made it to 3.4.20 ALL AND EACH INTACT.
New generation 1.1.2017 is LEAD the work.

william went up in the yellow helicopter and into into bright lights a world most affluent jungle
and biggest jungle and another'
series of computers and now mastered it. you learnt and you can drive.
our space workers have worked the hights and climbed throught the array. the world doing the
work got it right, the foundry to results which get our planet into a secure future for all aboard.
we had been planning it 20 years.
the worlds work is 16 years of planning, consumated.
there has never been an event before the work has never been done before. the instruction is made
in 3 900 languages and in computer access in every part of the world. the new computers reticale
in 2 days. and any delay
is overseen in 2 weeks therefore the passage is 2 weeks. and build plus
2 weeks return. how the world was won. borders are recovered. the borders of scotland collapsed.
huge amount of work is being done.
the passage in jesus time was 2years plus 2years return. the passage in leutenant cook scientific
mission times was 6months plus 6 months return the work was done on a lap top my book is
"from a lap-top"
we have book 1
    book 2
    lifes story
    lifes story 2
    document 1980-2020

drew family tree
11 memorial
museum in japan
tanks 5 presidents in a row . new mueum.
archive 45 000 to go in glebe bay floor.
briefcase II for Conference II
there is 0 response the number of people at begun enforcements 20 november 2020 are not
included in the production of genesis model known as genesis berth are through.
the guilty are defended by revolution the information from revolution work, calculation has got
the full number of the citicens through. first ever in the world
and the worlds first fair trial full 3 years to encounter evidence a world sucess.

i sign off you cant have any more story, it is the most story possible we wish you enduring sucess.
the world of 8 000 000 000 citicens is vastly enhanced.

EXPERTS IN PLACE

i have met my obligation boss of world to have an expert in place each time
i have met my obligation as owner philip and lalaine to have an expert in place each there has
been passage for 5 years from 2014 the passaged could be stalled corona virus actions, the rules
will still be able to get around as have independent facility.
the bosses travel in dominion will still be possible as dominion is an indepedent era and facility.
extraordinary travel could be secured by quote lucis estaban 35m
in columbia at this time . columbia was locked down march 2020.
your meeting is important and with lockdown quaratine or self isolation
cant happen.the foriegn minister must sign of. we treat the foriegn minister being in location as
urgent, the other ministers should do thier schedule.
for the work of the nations the foriegn minister of russia signed off. all is good. for you boris didnt
sign off julie couldnt be in place the new is woman.
ireland are innocent in 2013.
we have met our obligations and have 0 obligation, we have met the obligation of business plans
BP'99 BP200.
hays and philip are still the youngest in the business
we have seen the oceans of the world built and the computers which run our precious world built
and up and running and the world
workforce grown and documentation for communities and additional worthwhile funding. philip
and lalaine have funders we dont look
for an apply from any nation in the world and at this time
each business is in proffit. my empire made 8470 proffit. each business made a worthwhile
outcome.
the costs of event to us is >200b

the cost to nations is 1/3 economy so far.

any monies settled will increase proffit after taxations is settled.

any monies settled willprovide for dictate distribution creditors primary and weekender intact store. as instruction a cheque reciieved is to be made at the front counter. the world close nations built the

array and the computers leased to westpac the world uses westpac computers

and gay did the alignments. it has been up and running for some time sucessfully. you are

an evolved country australia. also port botany was sucessfully built. there has been vast environmental lands and showcased is queensland.

if america can put man and woman at home on mars america will make another vast fortunes.

saudi arabia and relation is the longest in the business

16 centuries and make fortunes. england is the next longest in the business

14 centuries and make fortunes the 3rd fortune, we got rich from coal, constant and theresa may 2019. sydney airport runs to 2029. sydney airport is the first private international airport sold off by the former owner

the government australia, samoa - the first privitised airport needed work.our

countries are starting out and had 0 money constance region funder has changed our world. we work hard. the office is in hong kong, the world meets.

the information is installed in immunion 9 and run the world.

pa and pa have screended the supply and has survey the message a second time to 191 new countries 35. my staff have built an office in each 191 countries and we hope to have the office completed 2022.

i own the furniture furnishings and the lobby on philip and lalaine books and the seniors 60 alfa romeo spider. and the furniture furnishings

in our existing offices. we own all the contents of emerald palace

me and my nunn. our decendency is a harem fully armed. we recovered the borders using helicopters the helicopters can carry 120 troops and evacuate 120 people i run 2 helicopters in each airorpt. we can maintain borders the each helicopter has enough firepower to consume half a city

and we did so maintaned the borders . the world owns the helicopters

and equipment world utilage, the people whom did the work contributed to saving 2 billion lives and we blew up the borders behind us so agressive arms

cannot cross. the nations supply the firepower. thank you for your help. thank you for paying, those whom paid have also defended animals as well as precious lives, my staff were awarded for saving the most number of lives in the

world, our precious world of 8 000 000 000 people the world we love.

my staff work in an office and not a warzone unless a defeated warzone. the fortitude is for the people whom work in a war zone.

exciting news to share.

Tutenkumun the embly of the resurection is in heaven in eternal life, the proceedure the resurection is in cairo after a big work and grace, the benefactors are adored for thier production, the body the benefactor of the much loved boy king has lasted more than 3000 years and is everlasting as planned. so are the

other kings whom have lasted more than 3 000 years an everlasting life. tutenkamen was sent to cairo from the lourve france in the tutenkamen exibition new york melbourne, paris has the deeds in hall. geoffry robertson was there in service and for england philip was in prescence. you were there and the time, world testables were on dvd tv and television. we were present whence julia bishop was in iran which is vastly celebrated.

like 2000 years before the world will read your testables in 2000 years to come and some will study your testables and line from your chronicles.

we are glad to be a part of a worthwhile world. one day jesus will come back

but there is only a 50% chance he will come back within 2000 years but make matter, be ready and have all you work up to date prepared distributed, loved ones kissed and prepared. you will glide up with your pharoah. our world is a universe

each kingdom has a dedicated pharoah.god will recieve the pharoahs people. TRUE. Revealation shows god will go past his pharoah and reckognise you.

if you want a life abide with your good sheppard. the ordinance retired at 88. the world 8 000 000 000 people children represented will judge you by whether you do the constitution and the acts. have it done so noone is let down.

this is called conscious. the majority of our citicens are bhuddist and will go to heaven with there pharoah, not you pharoah. we are all upset the schedule

of the church and traditions and monasteries are affected is ruined by

flights closed or self quarantine 2 weeks and cannot

be on time. we are upset when people are laid off including our people. it is sad but one benefit we get our economies are protected at a time we will be better off. we dont hope you last because you would have to

be embalmed but we do hope you have strength. the number of corona virus cases have gone down in china. it came in a lower supply line and aboard cruise ship. the work is to as you call it flatten the curve. we continue to work with

the ambition everyone is comfortable aboard. the pods are built at melbourne

a 3d graphic education . kay cottee vessel is at anmm. coal power stations now have a 400 % increase efficiency with black coal like adani and water manifolds like indias new power stations and low footprint on supply path and chain. in time india with experts will also build nuclear power stations. the

new power station is natural gas and will exceed commitments. nuclear far exceed

commitments you have no nuclear a long running and sustained campaign, also solar not nuclear the outcome is no nuclear. power stations are 30% of your emmisions and supply 150 % of your energy needs a profound and generous

achievement. growing needs are catered for by wind solar 50% of new build. we insist you do nothing you are far past achievement

the achievements global emmisions are 50 % less

in 50 years. agriculture is 33% and supplies 250% and exports money a profound and generous achievement. we recomend a new model cow for the other 33% we recomend a new model human.

the european countries have signed up to a further 40% per cent reduction.

Each country is a participent, news to celebrate. remember to say your thank you. finish of the work, we were paid handsomely.

the revelation is handsome. were going on the same model.

we recommend reduction in. we recommend positive control of antibiotics is the higest priority and where the most achivement is needed. england needs a 3rd invention or loose strenght sustain with less monies due to response to event.

we recommend cease the expansion of christianity as the enforcements, controls. we recommend delay the extension of christianity as the enforcements, controls. enforcements begun 20 novemember 2020 equal to diagram 2018. the race gets councells laid at windsor. remember to do your thank you. we got here because of your love

and penecillons and antibiotics. we did the signature and made file at hard rock cafe the lower boundary love all serve all, what you do. the treasure memorabillia

elton john hall the pinball wizard 1976 is the middle of the hard rock cafe makati. axle donated his white harley davidson is at hard rock cafe surfers paradise . i know the people whom opened hard rock cafe. i dont know any of the founders it is before i was born charity had interest in starbucks. its too american for me.

we founded new in existing relationships the quality is not cut. england give high quality of the highest in the world but charge the premium price. when

australia addressed the price and competitive edge didnt go down but only the wages went down and with exploded levies and impounded taxation the price is going up

with out any wage remedy a minority numbers in wage repeal. we have beat all the delaying decisions. i am a smoker and know how much repeal there is. our fortunes are much.

i was on the board of ramada and a member of the board, astoria. the best.

a perfect model to work from. I am an proud member of astoria and i love it, i love it.. we used to play pinball across from the high school at the milk bar when we were 16. when i did appointments i brought my steak dinner from the milk bar and all

around australia, brought the lamb cultlets, had bacon and eggs for breakfast when i was away and my favourite are tasmanian scollops, i had prawns

\3 times a week and chinese neal - western, hong kong 2 times a week. i ate at my favourite resturant and did all appointments at reasturants. when i grew up mum and dad ate at chinese resturant 2 week and club each sunday, dinner with friends saturday night and clubs served lobster and clubs when away.

i had lunch at clubs when away each day and dinner with friends saturday night. when lalaine immigrated we did an asian recipe each night and had a glass of wine with dinner. when we had to cut i cooked meal each night for 3 years . it was

good meal we passed our blood test for trace vitamins elements and i gave

no one food poisoning. lalaine had snacks at novatel. Every meal i eat is with vegatables and stir fries and thai curry has vegetables. i have lived an active life. my grandfather lived to 93 and many people asked him how he got to an old ages.

in his years he used to tell i eat carrots every day and also carrots will stop you going blind. my grandfather and granmother loved thier vegetables and ate vegetables

whites greens yellows every day. my granmother too lived to an old age. women didnt want to lead away from home women were courage and leadership in thier own home in another word from in theyre own home it is what the women wanted to do not the matter the women didnt have rights.no one could move them from there home and to run a farm

this is what happens today. it is the best thing to run a home and raise a family

not because women were made to stay at home but because it is what the women foremost wanted to do and it was the same in the part when i grew up. mum had a huge kitchen with a kitchen table in it and still had a big dining room and with the comfortable loungeroom this was the centre of the world by choice and believe it or not had a top model kingswood. stunning. mum and dad wanted a life in the suburbs and knocked back the other two lifes. mum and dad wanted a life in the suburbs and nothing else no other life attracted them

and most fortunately mum and dad had a superb life in the suburbs all theyre lives. theyre close friends were rich and a real nuclear family. yes nuclear family existed

and were profound. church was a delight and the cup was profound. believe it there was understanding. mum and dad went on holidays every school holidays and ate at favourite resturant and met at the club sunday half the time. mum cooked in to live the fun

half the time and had the excotic appliances. i became a fan of appliance and am a big fan of refrigerator, later i beacame a fan of electronics and have every electronics released to 2012. i went overseas. i brought a fridge toaster and the worlds most superb speakers shockwave for the house. we brought a tv . the tv is made of plastic

and can drop it, can even drop down a flight of stairs and it wont break, guaranteed, and a lifetime guarantee relied the salesman, made in the philippines like the fridge and air coolers. the english or big electric stove was like

owning a rolls royce. in the country a house has a wood stove. in the stove was a jacket . the hot water. plumbing was a new thing. aunty vera had a double oven simpson fabulous next to thier wood stove . my mother thought it was the revolution of the decade.

stove repairs was a big ticket. electricity suppliers had a big home cooking

centres and in penrith and the showrooms in australia. each were free and attracted a big crowd and plenty of students. this is where i started as an electrical apprentice the 2nd job in my 2nd career. in a huge family each of the husbands loved the wife. in 20 years cinamen and i loved each other and had good times, i never laid a finger on cinamen and so our family a large family each loved each other our world we did because we wanted to a far cry away from battery. australia faces a big problem with battery also with suicide. dont let it be you.. on my 18th birthday i got my drivers

licence and have driven over 1 500 000 km. australia faced a big problem with

road accidents.when i was 16 a best a best friend died at bathurst when his motorbike hit a truck. at 16 a best friend was on the train in the granville disaster when

the bridge fell on the carriage. every trip was always a big trip. every one in our family and friends drove a holden or america import and mum and dad has also a valiant and a datsun 240K a beautifull car. i learnt to drive on the datsun 6 cylinder manual and the huge valiant auto

and a tractor and learnt to ride a motor bike, later i learnt to drive a truck and use my hr licence to drive electrical rig first bedford acco the latest and best and entirely evolved from the bedford isusu beautiful brakes powerfull diesel 7 speed gearbox and superb ergonomics and seat. the country was full of bedford trucks . for

endless yaers the best and powerfull imported from england . exclusive cars from england was triumph austin humber . a mate described the old days, if you drove a jaguar you had to be truly rich. our country still depends on getting around by land like america.

other countries are built to go on foot. our country was built around the motor car.

in the country you do the longest distances and on dirt roads. the rairoad was the biggest spend and employed the biggest workforce per capita. 1888-1960.

. i had 27 years of holden v8 grand tourer and i went all over half

the country doing engagements.every time i did an engagement i went to the beach. australia spent a fortune in petrol

and were real petrolheads the way the country was designed.

we then brought a new generation gt. lucis brought a gt and went to new zealand we brought lucis car. lalaine decided on a bmw we sold after 3 years a immaculate sports car. for all the miles we do it is worthwhile for us to buy

sports cars. the bently the top of the line sports car in england in australia

is an hsv maloo ute the top of the line sports car and sought after. my nieghbour has a bently continental coupe but it doesnt attract the attention a ute does it just attracts my attention. For everything we needed

to do we had to drive or get a lift or take a limousine or cab. for everything we wanted to do we had to decide wether to drive or not go. for business today it is the same. in asia i did 200km a week on foot. at sydney airport i did

14 km a day on foot. i have done more miles on foot than most people in

the world and still done endless miles in a motor car or truck so have we all. i met a man who drove a road train . now the speed limit in the nothern

territory is 120km/h. i meet a man who lived in the mountains of america

who spent 3 months in cabin surround everynight by bears. he came to australia to

help his brother rebuild the fence on his farm after a bushfire. i met a billionaires daughter who has been rockclimbing for two years around america hanging from a thread before she goes back to her studies.

if you break down you have get past the preditors and the risks. over the years is built an automobile association.

The roadhouse diner and truckstop is popular.

THE big holden sells for double the price of a mercedes overseas. the gto

in california sold for the biggest money. a mercedes sells for double the price in australia. the bmw have specials and are the most popular.

the alpha romeo the most wanted car are the dearest and therefore when it comes to paying the money the least popular. the big holden when it came to production most people couldnt afford . people were not buying thier top models and were down

on sales. there are many cheaper cars . the big holden and the big petrol has died and so has the bathurst 1000 with ford the only competitor.

the supercar races go on and i guess holdens place will be won by jaguar an excotic car. the nieghbours has a jaguar and the nieghbour has a new ferrari gt but few can afford excotic cars. the other nieghbours have porsche boxter and range rover mercedes 300 mercedes roadster lexus 300 and cars about 100 000 and

a few nieghbours have a small car one nieghbour has a 1960s mini and a vw campervan, the old relic is worth 70 000., a mercededes gt and the nieghbours about 1/3 have a second car in the residents carpark..you can trip the city on the monorial

now trams after 30 years of the monorail and cross to manly on the ferry. to get off you need a licence and to stay you need a fishing licence.

the we bumped it up with ships going all over the world.

the monaro is built in england at a new factory.see top gear 40 . a car is a bargain compared to the price of a boat. A coles truck is bigger than the manly

ferry. my great grandfather and grandmother opened the first chain stores in australia. stock stores. the carrington hotel was opened with a steam laundry and the

first electric generators in australia giving the 7 star hotel electricity. now we eat in to stay out of virus. the next person whom writes your story will be someone from the future. god bless you.

Archive 2

MY CAREER IS SINCE1976

PLAIN

food glorious food more eggs and custard. beautifull england
lebanon in the holy biblw as described as a land flowing with milk and honey, delightfull table

all the countries have built beautifull food tracts. australia grows more food the australia and the islands
need and serves others in the world giving food on
thier table to a much larger number of people is the plan because astralia is the big land. we have already grown
and to improve our production we would have to build irrigation. it can be done and the supply is now much more
cost effective a desalination plant. per quanta a desalination plant is cheap and a low carbon footprint. you
will make a substatial bigger contribution to the world for equivalent carbon footprint and bless a large
number of people. new zealand has increased trade for similar footprint. food glorious food, beautifull
england does include sheep plus many other surprises. the agriculture also includes food for livestock and animals. the birds of the air have a lively feast but arent in the payment chain.
you should in aggregate reduce carcenegenics. you must achieve posotive penicillon and antibiotics ministration including animals and live stock. i donate to rspca. as small 35 each month which is
the rspca donators programme.there is already one dam has a bug in it. the overflow of dams wash the algie out of rivers . you must plan for drought so there is enough and have banked enough money to last all the way through the drought . the basic business model. use the information from beaureau of meteorology to plan your way through a drought.
you would get plenty of support from other nations we would think and lasting support.

thank you team george delightfull good

29

terrible the engagements region, nations, meeting, will not do an appointment in person, write to members
of appointment time date where be at apointment in person
and do appointment in person and do cheques in person and make sure cheques are done and issue is completed
and do follow up in person 20 - 30 minutes

we have met o monies appointments
in 2020 we have met 0 monies apointments
the balance 1.6.2020 is
182 000
167 000
65-72 643 000   of   4 020 000 000 000
                 2 200 000 000
                 156 000
                 400 000

the members of nsw politicians girls relyd signed the cheques club
another women problem in australia.

it is not possible to get a result when there are so many problems the world got the work right but cannot get a result. when
there is more work done there is thence more problems.
the enforcements are the only steady which can be supplied the innocent are vindicated at 6 years.
at 5 years there is 0 response
at 6 years there is 0 response why the world get cranky.
the results existed because the offense was controlled is the conclusion.

here is half the picture in one writing, the compass in 6 reports
these are 4 reports
the full picture is built from identity.

these are the world testables 1980-2020
nations records 2020
STORE

pink book teresa may
boris johnson did not do signature
scotland did not alarm weapons distater no 4

o citicen of england york scotland.

isolated
TWO GREAT MINDS, A LEAST WE LIKE TO THINK EACH HAS AN INDIVDUAL
SIGNATURE. I COULD BE BEHIND THE REPORT IS UP TO DATE, THE NATIONS
INFORMATION IS UP TO DATE.
COMMUNION
720 000 000 000 NOTES SPENT

HAYS 360 000 000 000 DAD ABRAHAMS 80 000 000 000 SPENT 2000 FUND

SURVEY, Maroubra Ocean Geographic Land Continent
Land boundary Trig beacon hill
australia, brothers, people whom live on islands SURROUNDS, BOUND to africa shore. there is
o nautical miles east of australia.
look see the content component and co ordination quality
of the work even at this age i have done it 59

CHART

cinamen daniel kerry 2 lucis ive, denomination, frank sartor, paul high, bobb carr world. george
mother becky, joanne humphries. kerry 2 a second time donna pascal banking manager,
30 000 royalties. bruce kathy bronwyn bishop. whip. stephen button. 0 writing from annette
doel the writing done 2010-2016 - 0 rely. rule ruled out is graphic less than protestent.2014
the verse was on 2014-2016 i dont understand what this means. pink book. rory, alan. alan,
wife, heather. heather schebol. anglican church paid in full, nsw cabinet lecture. bondi james
packer margaret children. my nieghbours in the philipines gave lalaine margaret packers flower
arrangement book as a moving in present. gift vince years /time in australia- time = 0 lucis sister.
treaty wen. peter angel cherry in australia
world underwriter, cherry in taiwan on tour in australia. male and girlfriend on university ground
darlington. serves. chart at university hall, professor bartholemew. howard children . john whom
finished, jeanette. bobb blanch paul a first
time. kim beazely. maybee these blokes got the work done because the blokes did understand the
work / it is the production. the production does exist. rose son. the old bloke died. this was our
first ground work in yhe country. alan bond . niel and family mother father. david soper charles
austin woods
the 3 prime minister study did not do there supply.windsor is in attendence.
0 below windsor cabinet 2 no triage perth no

intact governor of nsw 2015.
signature at edgeciff 2000 14 years 0=dead 0 atrocities.

the people name are not forsaken by the worlds actions and there signature witness and testimony is fluent

more. billionaire from london whom brought steelworks and whyalla. malcolm drinkwater, wife. john wife daughter son minto abercrombie. attendent black range rover. supply to

siagon publishing. witness to william going up in helicopter into bright lights, narrow neck.

brian malouf gail tammyy adam. kim lee.the children. party at signing william fukishima. passage guns n roses chinese democracy tour.

now we have a trien of australians.

philip attendent rose

roslyn charles staff. henry. accountant hazel brook. name bruce e lawrwence. party, julie bishop in iran, not julie bishop julie did not do her wrting. geoffrey robertson in egypt. 2 ships pass cowper wharf road. tower melbourne barry wife, boy post with buck teeth . the people whom are done, passage sixty years figures 2 men in china hamish. two men in a tinne

timeless roy hg. pfrofessor ian. head asio. grant. quenton, bryce,

the boss. penny wong. original labor woman perth, partner.george, girlfriend. we gave our gift to matilda.phil coperburg.

as you can see half my people are women. so it is in world, so it is in region. go post. the postal has been tested. warrant issued by geneva.

2 supply darwin berth, 2 cabinet no. rowena heather. radio rowenna

china mainstay control. westpac computers. vodaphone leases. sarina,

sharon. dad abrahams hays ken and barbie ken kerry 1 ian. sue samuels, sue gerome.

paul 0 test 6' tall. sydney location board laid. singapore submarine base jet location. wharehouse indonesia. office plain png. attache russia. we dont have a song

dr kay plain dr done plain. dr ian tait wife . dr bounds wife . friend

dr boundary westmead childrens hospital rspca proper. north syndney nsw health hall.

new operating theatre. union labor party.

plastic doll. hrh hmh hmrh officials seats and models windsor, her majesty has one third power in india we accept witness rely supply testimony testable from journal india, i get my supply from journal india. and journal, journey asia pacific region and asia pacific region corum, space asia. 100% and intermediate supply, in journey, nations councells. logs. attendence logs, immediate inspection. we accept her majesties supply at the end of after 6 years the race get councells because of launch on iran

and increase on north korea and reltion countries we do not accepet england york scotland united states, amrica race supply. in 2014 2015 we got united states america to writing in the 2nd continent rule usa the 2 rule wog job. 10am 2pm. all systems go son in law son in law lead. america is instucted porting out of hawaii.

100 per cent of the rebel are dead and there is to be no further incise america country is to leave, the bombings 2020 can be maintained any bombings against england have a licence since actions 2014 north korea has finished flooding in the

14 european nations farmland radiation poisoning. manymar must not purge against muslims. each other country must not purge against muslims. indonesia must not purge into muslims. indenesion should purge. there is immunion.

we also accept the testimony of englad concord.

more shall be advised. searches equal 0 . i have done searches by each searcgh a huge workload.

but england got i across the line .

we accept the assemblies in the new generation thank and those in one organisation in anglican united, methodist and australia catholic communion

and dont accept the evidence of australia catholic parishes.we accept the relys from the outcomes of royal commision. we accept the rely of high court philip

did bench in 2015. we accept the governor of nsw documents 2015 account. we accept my philip order, we accept philip lucis record.

we accept lalaines ives. we accept rosalinas ives. we accept kieth doel

jan doel closure. uncle kieth and aunty jan with a crew drove a tractor

4000 miles to perth to raise publicity for the work the world ethic and we have had plenty of staff installed, thank you very much.

each person in the world has benefits. the benefits each person has has been grown. if someone dies the benifits are overshadowed by

a reprocussive problem. the work to save a life is done 17 times in the world. the worlds work is now done twice hense there is sufficient work done in every and each case. congratulations.

we accept congressbenching. we accept laid copenhagen holland

ireland

we accept as record berths records warsar room rome.

vaults chicago.

asi werrington. we dont accept industry computers or pacfic delta power. we accept castlereagh st.

we accept philip monarc vault behind library.

we accept library floor. this is the work done.

i did engagements and additional work and we raised 23 550 000

we raised 2 221 000 in 4 accounts

income 205 000

438 000 invested. REPAIR34 000 000

REPAIR34 000 000

the foundry work was 156000

the annual fishing competition beefed up got in 0.5 billion dollars

for australia, equal to the largest project. we built the space

and my staff did the space work.

there are good and substantial results.

australia environs australia surrounds is planned differently today

than when the castles were built. without war the conference,

despite there has been wars, the governor generals head of office

and quarters has no revel forces. at the governor nsw there is

still revel forces and in 2015. the prime ministers quarter is

supply from the prime minister quarter because the prime minister travel to canberra 50 percent of security is from ships out

to sea and is better security fo the islands. 50% of staff

former revel forces have served have been passage,

my passage the ward. the governorgeneral has new quarters.

you can visit the old places. mr malcolm moved to syney harbour

we did our best to order supply.we cant move the people staff back again.

the people in charge of the kingdom now have theyre own place

instead of attention at the castles. in the internal which is the number

of citicens each has its own name. to a foriegner of planning war

it is castle like the other places of 45 000 kingdoms in the world.

the plan for the slavage coming up to war went to elizabeth II castle. for the citicens it is called

windsor and windsor berths. the

salvage is the fauklands war . the next time is coming out of

the gulf war. the next time is gerth 2013. you can read the

picture and history wikepeida page the british empire. i have

for a long time worked for the british empire and at this time i am

not allowed supply as a boss because i might be biased for england.

i the work i have done for england i am but the supply for nations

is intact and pure. the work is sucessfull england has grown in

communities and made fortunes. 140 countries migration

hong kong 2006. 1 kingdom.53 commonwealth countries.

see wikipedia page post office.

european today is 121 countries.

MY CHEMICAL ROMANCE ARE THE WORLD 120 COUNTRIES SOLIDARITY

ARMED FORCES> known as 120

CHEMICAL ARE THE ARMED FORCES OF THE COMMUNIST COUNTRIES.

ROMANCE IS THE ARMED FORCES OF THE DEMOCRACY COUNTRIES.

RUN FROM THE TOP, THE NEW BULID IN THE WORK AND SUCESSFULL SERVICE I

DEVELOPED THE LONG MENTAL HEALTH BOARD

AND WE HAVE MEDALS AND WERE GIVEN AWARDS.

I RETIRED SERVICE 2016

RUSSIA IS A PRODUCING DEMOCRACY 6 YEARS. ROMANCE.

SHORES AND BORDERS HAVE BEEN DONE FOR THE BALANCE

OF COMMUNIST COUNTRIES. THE COUNTRIES HAVE BEST

RESULTS FOR CITICENS. MEDICARE IS A BEST RESULT>

PHILIPS RETIRENMENTS ARE

2000

2000

2004

2005

2006PLAIN PNG

SEAT AFGHANISTAN PLAIN.

REVOLUTION PAKISTAN. the completion war against terrorism.
The assaination of bin laden proved by denture dna completion documents.
The launch of pakistan nation communications satelite, tower
Our people and troops flooded behind USA 14 years.
North korea include japan flooded 14 years supplying 14 countries
after chenoble accident the one third of the farmland
radiation poisoned. the two big effort in the world
COMMERCIAL-writer WRITING 2008 passaged
COMMERCIAL-writer SUPLLY 2009 PASSAGED
nice men in black garments heavily weapon loaded
the passage come to pick up the volumes 12,14
passages in 2008 and took all the work for the world to terrain
and laid the work carefully, the peoples working from
the work came in, in 2009 passages took all the work, supply.
we posted away and posted all over the world we heard back
when each posting was laid and ticked off work.
the writing scotland in 2011 was laid.
SUCESSFULL COMMERCIAL -Writer
2010
2013 philip ran the world 6 biggest developements
Developements completed july 2013
2013 resigned from company
STAYS 5 Presidents in a row
20.11.2013 work no t completed
monies disordered
2014 actions by nations, INSTRUCTIONS
2016 INSTRUCTIONS
2015 organisations run by new owners, fully serviced
2018 books
2015 RETIRED FORMALS
2015 RETIRED FORMAL
RETIRED BERTH. installed, Head of Asio Retired.
2016 RETIRED SERVICE, COMPLETED SERVICE
2016 MY PEOPLE COMPLETED SERVICE
Retired scientist
2017 retired manual work.
2020 Lalaine retirement.
2020 retirement monies is stolen from our bank account hk1
in transit.
2020 sale 205 000 of 6 properties to live in and office of
11 properties.
2024 sale 242 000 foot 59

infection.

banking 360 000 000 000 costs 220 000 000 000

140 000

460 000

2018 RECIEPT KINGDOM THEY 300 000 000 000 000

berlin pay 360 000 000 000

philip pay 4 200 000 000 000

       1 600 000 000

inheritence hays 360 000 000 000

elizabeth extraordinary pay.

annette pay 0, annette deny

ramada board paid

astoria board paid

staffer philips corporation belgium holland paid.

anglican church paid to 2004.

lalaine paid 10%

family 86 000

2000 2020cinamen creditor

2020 vince creditor

charity paid up

lucis paid.

distribution 0

dictate paid to 2015

bayswater settlement stolen.

books for england daniel.

books matthew.

Workplace HERE

EMPLOYER

PARTNER

annette was pay 0 annette did 0 writing in each one case
if monies were stolen there were still billions of
dollars to work from. for mother the distribution
monies were stolen . books uncle.
samuel and lydia monies were settled and completed
at rooms burwood.
for the members doel some monies were settled or
more for each had a mansion.
royalties were paid.
when philip the monarch was in charge, england all
monies were paid and settled the new generation 2000
england the monies are missing before 2000 england

had a perfect histoy with monies we have a perfect history.
for the members taiwan the settled monies were stolen.
over to intelligence, whom did the crime.
wherein we have monies stolen there have been and
billions of dollars to work from and work with,
we have met all of our commitments.
we still have money in ausralian accounts and
22 000 000 in england account.
we are low on money in currency in accounts
we can draw from 2010-2020 291 000 PA in 2000-2010
353 000PA we made it. we have plenty of money in
accounts we insruct from
and 3 owners earnt 1.6b into personal bank accounts.
2020we are 1.6 b clients
donald trump is ditributed is is 3.5b
englands surveyor richard branson is
through the roof. richard is having trouble
however from corona virus.

mr abrahams is the wealthiest as he was,
a funder. i worked with each leader.
harry was the richest person now gina.
england has consistently worked with gina.
jessica watson is the person of greatest award.
the person of award was 2 times winner of
wimbledon, florida maria sharapova.
our hall and your high awards
was hall cantebury at
hall canterbury leagues club assembled
by philip kidd the original awards
made by the award winner by donation.
one award winner wasnt available, the
also held the original award, plate
to pharlap, kay cottee the first
woman to sucessfully solo-circumnavigate
the globe. kays boat is on display in the
australian maritime museum pyrmont also
know as darling harbour, sydney,
steve mortimer installed. philip and
steve are mates, serving members in the
football club member since 1982.
my staff did the space for

jessica watson solo circumnavigation
and 2 intended rescue out of chilli,
bound chilli and off chilli.
the international border 1 rescue
and in the 2nd rescue the navy chilli
didnt touch jessica boat even tho
the boat urgently needed stablising.
the family bit thier fingernails
jessica stayed at the helm. our staff
gave her instructions to counter the
helm. it is true jessica or jessica boat
was never touched by a person. i am
the head and made the raceline. the
first weather was bad. the second
weather situation was severe.
jessica just made it. kay had a whale
surface on her boat half way around
the circunavigation. jessica would
be disqualified if a person touch
jessica orthe boat in the rule
of the race, jessica wanted to persist,
i wrote off a 16 year old but equal to
her specification jessica made it,
jessica was out of breath so was my
staff and the sea rescue.
jessica made it home to
the dock sucessfully an
australian the youngest women in the
world to sucessfully circumnavigate
the globe, jessica was 16
we do the space each year for
the sydney to hobart yacht race
each year i went aboard
wild oats 4 the 4 times line
winner. i started off in the
sucessfull americas cup
challenge, alan bond, ben lexen.
i ran the rescue vessell
for ian murray challenge
australia 2 but we we
unsucessfull. all good times.
i have been in yacht racing

since i was 23. i built
the helm australia berth
the royal motor yacht club,
charter, sydney, berth sydney
harbour with my staff
an aeronautical which spans
one third of the globe.
these attributes help keep
people safe at sea and get
work done.
i played golf 38 years.
i body surf and we love
dancefloors in our years.
i have also done music
and for a time a music
retailer and for a time
a record company stooge.
i have been a boss since 1996.
and owner since 1976.
my first career.
i am a sucessfull commercial writer.
my second career to supply
home 1980-2000
my 1st career continues with
philip and lalaine at the
helm. our business plans
are fully serviced in 2015
and run by seniors and
head of staff. ourstaff
philip kidd space are
leading experts and do space
and switching all over the
world. my staff were awarded
for saving the most lives in
the world 3 era in a row.
i did not deny and was
promoted and has been
a long serving boss
of the world. each work i was
given i did a good job and i
was promoted< we have
seen sucess.

with the new arterials and
reticultions built the
australian navy has rescued many at sea,
the region people have rescued
many at sea. the drones donated by
america installed the
region people has saved many
lives. thank you for your
participation.

in the end we have books.
in revelation we see at time, the books were opened!
this will include your grace, love.
the asia pacific region, our love is a light.
many commands at sea are run from
the new suburb in space we have a joint
command centre which is big and has a
big floor we built with china and is in
china also chinas robot on the moon a worlds
first was sucesfully landed on the moon
from the command centre mission centre.
and some australians workin the
controll centre we work with,
head office is in japan.
philip and lalaine are region, region.
\philip is rocketman. philip was
the former asia pacific region
technical and at the confidence of
the rulers and leaders of the countries
of the asia pacific region was
installed region. lalaine was accepted,
installed region. in 15 regions.
we are getting nearer to a rocket and
we are excited. it is appropriate to
our patience to our scientists as our
scientists work the long hours and
we will continue to lease 5 lauchsites
the region has done many launches and
one day we will have our own rocket.
rocket technology is the hardest of
all sciences to achieve and in
2019 a generation rocket blew up

carrying a payload to the space
station 500m from the launchpad
in america in a massive fireball
reliability even all these years
later is so hard to achieve. the
rocket is being replaced by the
manufacturing company russia free
of charge in the same model in
a second generation design, build.
the payload is being replaced free
of charge in our flooding in space
but has to make it to dock by
6 months, the race is on.
the national broadcaster has
all the goodly news, i watched
each event on television . for
the launch schedule you can
go to russia space .com which
is europe and england mission
centre. the mission centre was
for many years in england. now
it is in russia. work at the
space station is not a space
mission
but part of the work which run
the world. space work. space
is the
assetts owned by the 45 000
kingdoms
of the world meaning you.
you now have more equipment
out at sea which is used for
navigation response rescue
and saving lives. some of
the contributors are persons
whom are in yacht racing or
people like us whom do
space and funding for a living.
i have been a member of
canterbury since 1982, watched
every canterbury a grade game
foe 30 years and never missed

one game even though i spent
nearly a quarter of my days
away from home so good were
the days games were televised
on free to air channel where
you can dial in from anywhere /
i did the work with members
of cantebury. the archive is
a display hurlstone park
rsl club. like a sydney sider
i met with friends for dinner
every saturday night.
lalaine and i have been to
240 destinations in the years
we were abroad and had dinner
in 240 destinations. i have
had bacon and eggs for
breakfast every day i stay
away and cheesecake
and coffee for tea.
philip did 86 international
flights and lalaine did
46 international flights.
there are diplomatic embassies
i have done 1 400 000 kms by
road in australia. we have
done 120 000 km in asia and
200 km a week on foot. at
59 i wore my foot out. we
have lived in the
sub penthouse with lucis
7 years, and our home
has members. my new office
is fully built and spans
the planet. devotion by
nice people including
from your kingdom.

BALANCE SHHET 2022

Balance 2020   10 800
                                                16931
                                                167000
                                                65-72 643000
_____

MONIES PAID BY PHILIP AND LALAINE for Office 2012   3 068 000
_____

MONIES PAID BY NATIONS   FULL BOOKS

                    2014-2018   3 972 000 000 000
ORGANISATIONS   60 000 000 000 PA
AFRICA BORDERS   80 000 000 PA
Monies stolen   >10 200 000 000

                        INCOME   8470 PROFITT
                             ENTIRE EMPIRE
_____

WE WERNT MADE OUR SELVES CHILDLESS COUPLE FOR A PURPOSE WHICH
IS SELFISH WE MADE OUR SELVES CHILDLESS COUPLE FOR THE PURPOSE OF
DOING THE WORK.
PHILIP AND CINAMEN BUILT THE EMPIRE FROM THE GROUND UP AND DID THE
WORK.

1980-2000   28 000 000
                                2000 940 000 000
                                2000 22 500 000 STOLEN
                                    SETTLEMENT MONIES STOLEN
                                2000 75 000 PAY OUT

MONEY WE CAN DRAW FROM 28 000 000
940 000 000

PHILIP MARRIED LALAINE
LALAINES BOOKS ARE CALLED LALAINE IS A MILLIONAIRE

2000 - 2020
2002 SALE OF LEURA TO PAY FOR BUSINESS COSTS   2002   280 000
2000 - 2020   23 550 000

MONEY WE CAN DRAW FROM
Account England 22 000 000
2 221 000

2020   2020   2022   35 000
SALE OF BEACHOUSE TWO STORY APPARTMENT PACIFIC DRIVE PORT
MAQUARIE   205
000

4 000 000 000 000

MONEY WE CAN DRAW FROM
MONIES HELD BY REGION 161 000 000
190 000 000
STOLEN MONIES SETTLED STOLEN IN TRANSIT
205 000 less fees
34 000 000 STOLEN FROM BANK ACCOUNT
TRIAGES CHEQUES
156 000 DUE COUNCELLED

2022   CASH BALANCE   167 000
65-72 643 000

REPORT, THE REPORT IS CALLED IT IS A LONG WAY TO TIPPERARY
THE REPORT IS ALSO CONFERENCE, BOOK TO PUBLISHER, AND LAY
UNITED NATIONS NEW GENERATION OFFICE, BANKOK,
PART OF THE WORLD TESTABLES, RECORD. RECIEPTS FOR TAXATION CLAIM.
BOOK TO FRIENDS, ITERATED THANK YOU. NUMERAL IS FILE IN PDF FORMAT.
we are celebrating 40 years.

FUND 1966

Open   350
22500
25000 60 000 000
our first clients donated mature work
donation of fund, equipment nations
I DID NOT PAY FOR THE SETTLING OF EQIPMENT IN DONATION OF
FUND BY NATIONS OR JOINT

NATIONS
all taxations settled
I PAID 42 YEARS TO 2020
WE MADE IT IN 2020

MONEY IN THE PHILIPPINES   0.261 M COST
19.5 M
DEPOSIT 70 000
10

NEW GENERATION 1.1.2012
\AWARDS AWARDED DISTINGUISHMENTS MEDALS, CONTINUE TO PAY
VOLUNTARY STAFF 22 000

———————————————————————————————

———————————————————

STIPENDS PAID
INSURANCE = O
> 1400 CLAIMS PAID BY MUNICH INSURANCE
HISTORY INSURANCE = 0
0 = ACCIDENTS CREDIT = 0

———————————————————————————————

———————————————————

OWNERSHIP   CINAMEN
                             PHILIP
                             LALAINE
                             LIEGH
                             VINCE CREDITOR
                             CREDITORS 2000
                             CREDITORS 2020
                             OUR CONSTITUTION WORK PARTY
                             2015 NEW OWNERS, FULLY SERVICED
                             4 NEPHEWS

                             TOTAL INCOME PHILIP
                                    CINAMEN
                                       LALAINE
            1980 - 2020 CASH $ 1, 596, 856, 725 AUD IN BUSINESS BANK
            ACCOUNT\
            HELD 160 000 000 190 000 000 34 000 000 CANNOT BE
            CONCLUDED TO
BUSINESS BANK ACCOUNT,
            CHEQUES SIEZED, INTERNATIONAL COURTS
            SETTLEMENT, COMMONWEALTH
BANK ACCOUNT.
            ALL BALANCE OF OPERATION COSTS WILL COME OUT OF
            ANOTHER ACCOUNT.
            MONIES IDENTIFIED BY INVESTIGATORS 1500, SUPPLY TO
            BOSSES OF THE
WORLD.
            COMPUTER INPUT

AFTER ALL COSTS PAID AND TAXATIONS SETTLED
STOLEN   750 000
> 10 200 000 000 AUD MARCH 2000-2022,2026
5600 PERSONAL BANK ACCOUNT 1998
BUSINESS LOSS
TRIAGE CHEQUES 34 400 000 LOSS
BUSINESS LOSS SHOWN IN COURT RECORDS
REPORT

Balance = 0 BP ' 99 BP 2000
AUSTRALIAN BUSiNESS <5% LOSS 1982-2014
VOLUNTARY WORK SUCESSFUL 0% LOSS
LALAINE HAIR 0% LOSS
ENGAGEMENTS 41% PROFFIT
RUNNING 10 % PROFFIT
ATTRIBUTE 41% PROFFIT

2 CAREERS
SUCESSFULL COMMERCIAL-WRITER
PHILIP AND HAYS ARE THE YOUNGEST IN THE BUSINESS

IDENTITYS

WHITE
PHILIP KIDD SPACE since 1976
PHILIP KIDD ELECTRICAL AND INVESTMENT
IMPRESSION
CINAMEN 3500
CINAMEN AISLES GROUND GIRLS EFFORT BELLS PUB COWPER WARF RD BAY
BY THE SEA
ENGAGEMENTS
SIGNATURE
APPOINTMENTS FOR WORLD, KERRY II
ARMS SURVEYOR, QUANITY SURVEYOR, SPACE
WEAPONS SURVEYOR
Lalaine HAIR INVESTMENT
Lalaine OWN INVESTMENT II INVESTOR

INVESTMENT 4
Lalaine 15 Generations
CINAMAN COMMAND, DAD II
COMPOUND AND VATICAN POTTS POINT
PHILIP AND CINAMEN HISTORIAN
AUTONOMY, WORLD UNDERWRITER
APPRENTICE THENCE BOSS OF INDUSTRY, SALESMAN
POOL SALESMAN
PRODUCTIVITY SUPERVISOR, SALESMAN FOR BRITISH EMPIRE
LALAINE MIDDLE CLASS
LALAINE SURVEY OF ARMS BORN PHILIP BORN
PEACE PHILIP AUTHOR,
Office of Dignity
CONDUCT OFFICE CORAL SEA
DEPARTMENT OF FAIR TRADING LICENCE AND CERTIFICATE
OWNER OF BUSINESS, BUSINESS SALES MATURE INVESTMENT
BECAUSE OF NEW ALIGNMENT IN EVENT WE HAVE o JOB UNDER 3 B
I DO WANT MORE JOBS
MINORITY INVESTMENT
COMMERCE WORK FOR CLIENTS
SERVICE TO CLIENTS BOARD MEMBER

Region Region
DOCTOR OF IVES PHILIP KIDD DEAN CHUENG
COMMERCE BOARD 15 GENERATIONS, OWNER
EMPLOYER
PARTNER
DOCTOR BY STAMP
DOCTOR BY LINE OWNER
2ND CAREER, STAFFER
HAIRDRESSER AND MAKEUP ARTIST HR EXCECUTIVE CONTRIBUTOR
family Member
Head of Secret service, English Retired Scientist
Profile, Voluntary work
Overtime
WE HAVE GOT HALF OUR MONEY FROM INVESTMENTS, MOST OF THE MONEY
HAS COME FROM BUSINESS SALES

Personal income	1990-2000 Philip Cinamen 240 000 PA
	2000-2010 Philip 353 000 PA
	2010-2020 Philip and Lalaine 755 000 PA
	2020 2022 35 000
	HOUSEHOLD INCOME 2014-2022 $242 000 PA

EMPLOYER

ESTATE SETTLEMENT from BILL RUBY JOHN JANET, GIFT PHILIP PAID 40 YEARS, PAID RAISED AS A CHILD, FUND 1966

Contribution and monies paid by our friends in the WORLD ETHIC PARTICIPLE, Transit stolen Royalties, Disturbed

COMMISERATION FRIENDS, AND STEVE AND ROSE

\BBQ'S

From the corporate monies we have grown

From centre monies My Staff, People the developer Celestial Aligned with the Developer Celeste the years later

We are the worlds biggest biggest builder

THE KIDD family have done big developemnts, I have done developements as an inter-continnental developer,

and developements for the world. John Robert Kidd developed the European Line of Congress. I have done the signature and the SEAL. With my Witness we have Signed Sealed and delivered a PLANET.

I did 1 400 000 km in Australia we Did 120 000 km in Asia

We together also have many projects and equipment. As peoples we built and own camp across borders.

We have searches study and reasearch going i have a modern home office fully built which spans the planet.

\WE CAN MOVE THE OFFICE AND CHAIR TO ONE OF OUR 6 Properties to live in and office. My organisations had 473 properties

and now have 494 properties of which 11 are philip and lalaines properties and 6 to live in and office is some of

my work as the owner. All our numbers are recorded.

Lalaine runs our affairs. Lalaine has 0 liability. The favourite movie is shades of gray. Axle and guns and roses in person laid

all the deeds in chinese democracy tour. the world is on the same page. Love and Grace have seen the worlds biggest achiement. WE ARE HOUSE OF COCONUT + WOOD 2020

I KEEP ALL THE BOOKS
THERE ARE DIPLOMATIC EMBASSIES

CONCLUSION, EACH BUSINESS IS IN PROFFIT

WE ARE FORTUNATE, THE WORK DONE IS EXCELLENT WORK

THE 60 year figures are done for australia and laid is generous and compassionate work. HOBBY PURPOSE HAVE 19% Response.

IN EVENT AS BOSS I GOT REPONSE FROM 86% of the WORLDS POPULATION. A BETTER EQUATION THAN WE HAVE EVER SEEN BEFORE.

THE PEOPLE WHOM SIGNED THE WORLD BEFORE WHOM HAVE THE BIGGEST RESULTS IS, WERE AUNTY LEONIE AUNTY JANET PHILIP, GREECE

\PHILIP WAS MY FIRST EVER BOSS. DAWN CHAMBERS WAS MY MENTOR. IT IS MY OBLIGATION TO HAVE AN EXPERT IN PLACE AND

I HAVE AN EXPERT IN PLACE. AT THE END OF ALL MY STUDIES I HAVE ALL THE LICENCES. LALAINE HAS DEVOTION. CINAMEN

HAS THE LONGEST COMMAND IN THE WORLD THE RELAY OF EACH NATION BUILT OVER MORE THAN 75 YEARS. LIEGH HAS THE HIGHEST

DICTATE IN THE WORLD WHICH IS LIEGH 39, I HAVE THE HIGHEST INDICIE IN THE WORLD 48. IF England get Through Her Majeaty Elizabeth

is the Biggest contirbutor to peace in the world already voted. It took each person in the world in an world effort fortified by

england to make the world a better world, thank you for your life cheer work help fortified effort love and contribution.

Our passage is the Western World. I was installed as Boss in 1996. I have locked all the Corrupt Out. I treasure my relationships as a

member and I am a Grace Labor Party Global, Defender for the Victims, I ordered the Figures. I am a sucessfull commercial-writer.

Lalaine is immaculate, Lalaine is also beautifull, lalaine is a beautifull partner and we have had many experiences together.

we have 2 200 photographs. i have done 86 international flights lalaine has done 46 international flights. In engagements and

Signing we have been to 240 destinations and seen 120 sights of the region and raised 23 550 000 we met each invitation. We are

Region, Region, I AM ROKETMAN. I WAS THE FORMER ASIA-PACIFIC REGION TECHNICAL AND WITH PEACE BOSS OF THE

UNITED NATIONS ARMED FORCES SALARY, OWNER OF ELECTRIC LABORITORY WHOM DO THE SPECIFIC WORK FOR THE WHOLE WORLD AND A FULL SCALE NUCLEAR DIVISION WHOM DO NUCLEAR EMBATTLEMENTS ARTILLERY AND SCIENCES ALL OVER THE WORLD. I

NEGOTIATE WITH PRINCESS CHINA THE DEMONSTRATOR

OF THE COMMUNIST WORK. HALF OUR WORKFORCE ARE WOMEN. RUSSIA DO THE WORK IN MY SOLICITORS RUN THE SOLICITORS WHICH IS THE ARTICULATION

FOR THE WORLD. BY 2019 The World is Run by Generation, Triens, GIANT COMPUTERS JUNGLE SUPPLY MILITARY COMPUTERS.

BUILT OVER 35 YEARS. SUPPLY AND MANUALS ARE ON A SHIP. THERE ARE MANY PEOPLE AT IMPORTNANT WORK IN THE WORLD AND ARE OUT OF

OWN COMMUNITY FOR MOST HOSPITAL IS ABOARD ON A SHIP. WE DO WORK FOR THE VAST NUMBER OF PEOPLE AND HAVE DONE SPACE SINCE 1976.

EACH NATION AND UNIONS OF NATIONS HAS MADE A VAST CONTIBUTION TO THE BENEFIT OF EACH PERSON IN THE WORLD AND OUR SUPPLY CAN BE

IN EFFECT AND OUTCOME BETTER AND BETTER EACH TIME IS EXACTLY WHAT HAS HAPPENED AND WE ALSO DO THE LONGEST EDUCATION IN THE WORLD.

WE ALSO BUILD A FULL LENGTH PRESENTATION TO EACH NATION. WE ARE SINCE 1982. WE ALL HAVE SOMETHING TO GIVE AND Lalaine Put the Sisters

Through University. I have done 2 lifetimes and all my people are retired and are new people.

In 2015 I retired from formal aqnd formals

and Reaveal Whom is 100% of People to a new generation. 100% of Ally are Home travelled in Majaton or Rocketman our 10 BARRISTERS.

28 years after 911 the collapse of twin towers the Rebel is Dead Europes worst enemy and we do the Preceedure rebuilding ONE LOVE.

After 18 Years the nations have a result against england. I WON Hospitalice for My staff in PORTUGAL and my Staff has been in Portugal.

I GET Help With Staff Security For my Balance of staff and importantly I have to run my assets. I n The Work for the

WORLD lalaine and i worked through each decision and we got it RIGHT. Our work has run sucessfully. We live on the ocean boulevade.

On 30 . 3 . 20 Our 2 story beachouse appartment on the sands of flynns beach on the ocean boulevade pacific drive port maquarie 150m2 settled . our

379 435 after fees proffit and income 205 000. 1x1400 businesses we love and had 8 years. lalaine went with friends to manly beach. We hosted many years

with results in each nation. we were doing all the volumes of work all the way. the consumations of the citicens of the planet achieved

the biggest results in the history

our universe and made history and revelation. the monies was immediately and intentionally disordered. I was requested to give account

i was helped when the nations put 1500 INVESTIGATORS ON. I GET HELP WITH STAFF SECURITY.

Lalaine got councell. Lalaine has completed books.

There was response from 86% of the worlds population. The World saved 2 billion lives. we had wonderfull years. when we met and went out the people

had the time of thier lives and we had wonderfull times. good years. some of our time has been spectacular. we dont really live a quiet life we are

nice and good people and we always have commitments. our times were immemorial to our our loved ones and the people we love we were wild . the people meant everything to us and we loved our staff. we have sucess. wild. i have done writing most of my adult life.

have for a long time been the Boss. none have died with us in charge a confident and better world. Madonna is the world faith, praise her name, The pope and madonna have equal wins, with madonna there were an army of beuatifull confident girls

doing missions in the known part of the world with enourmous and lasting sucess, madonna and the girls is the largest private devotion in service

in the first effort. the girls had to be evacuated from africa when the blacks jumped the wall. the blacks killed and descimated the last of the cousins of

the propriety england york scotland and is the last installment of england. the girls whence we evacuated them wouldnt go home to united staes of america and we negotiated after

we gave the girls citenship in our region . later a service was built for the girls. the rest of madonna girls whom are now of great service abide in america.

the end of the old days . the region passaged 1 800 000 000 people from all parts of the world in the witness protection scheme,

whom we are to day. in our lifetime thier is a full information. the world over 75 years

has had more information to work from and has had extraordinary suceees.

madonna head of staff, is in the years after my region senior and reef my region senior and i work with the region seniors journey and seniors. the regions are built

in the world and we value australia solomon new caledonia and torres strait nation and new zealand concord new zealand

and maouri polenesian islands the region come first as you have done for many years and you are now experienced in doing.

you have saved many lives and our ocean graphics have saved many lives. my staff and lalaine owner was awarded in 3 era

3 times for saving the most number of lives in the world and won other awards . like madonnas girls and the other people in the business and the worlds own staff and the united nations salary and bill gates legacy and the survey whom run the oceans my people are nice people. competence has got the world so far. my next door niegbour was one whom ran the world keren was john paul, the most senior. my other

nieghbours ran communities there were more than 16, when we grew up the next door nieghbour was the mayor of 20 years,

MI6 was in charge. we had some teaching all the way. we have seen some milestones. dave runs the MI6 Fan Club. my

nieghbour at leura was mayor of lane cove for many years and a nieghbour leura owned an international fashion label.

it is all on dvd happy days. our next nieghbour as child owned the bakery a big business, when my mother was young my granfather

ran the largest bakery in australia and lived in the bakery house moved from the mansion in burwood. my grandfather did

pathways all his life. i was installed i have now finished, our other two nieghbours was doctorbell and denist whom were also famous horse breeders and races and winned some of the most cherished event in australia including in the melbourne cup

the tarcoola line. i learnt to play golf and won and played golf for 38 years, i was on the state tennis team. i later moved to

the blue mountains. lalaine grew up in a mature place . we were a middle class and lalaine was in middle class. at 14 i begun the business

. i was first orerdered as an entrepreur but the conducts grew beyond entreprenour into an empire, at 16 i launched philip kidd

space which is a multi billion dollars work. we went to the farms reguarly and stayed with

jan and kieth doel and went away on holidays with mum every school holidays

. we saw reguarly philip pearl jan lex brewer mum and dad were in business with bob and barb elison cecandmarie until marie was in the nursing home

lotti stewart hospital, they all had mansions and we had great days today we are

rich in our business and are middle class, the settlement for my new house was stolen i havent had a house since we cant make up the money. since we have had more money,

we have had a large amount of money stolen, i moved into the office.

i first moved to the boat on pitwater at newport.the traffic was too bad with the big bucks i moved into a hotel the number 1

living choice. when i lived in the blue mountains before i moved to sydney 2000 i stayed many nights at the cameo inn rose bay and the cameo inn closed after 20 years to be turned into appartments. i was lost\

for a place to stay andfound palm court and stayed there every night i was in sydney. i

spent nearly one quarter of my time staying away in australia. i did 1400000

km. lalaine and i have been halfway around asia. i body surf and we loved dancefloors, dancing. lalaine gives the good parents a middle class retirement. the farms

bring in 1 billion dollars crop per annum each farm if a crop comes home and supports 23 familys and supplies for 3 generations in 2019 is draught- commercial wheat farmers. lalaines granparents are commercial rice farmers to 88, Lalaines granfather step mother commerce board signed in authication the deeds for south america continent.

Lalaine was born in 15 generations. cinamen father was a significant commander, he educated me, he died very young of a heart attack the ones he left behind were distressed,

our people are remembered. my mate has a pacemaker at 36.

we not only wish you good life, times and benefit, but we wish you good health. the newsagent in rosebay showed me have to set up a share. i did the signing at edgecliffe

i have never been to edgeciffe before even tho it is just around the corner..since i have been to edgecliff many times but

the means is reticulation and the facility the telephone. my region staff have been to edcliffe to sign. ive watch most of it on tv. the work, information for the whole world is on dvd. the

6th biggest achievement in the world and the most gracious work. The worlds deeds are signed in person, axle rose guns n roses chinese democracy tour. we have signed sealed and delivered a whole planet, you have been represented faithfully. There are diplomatic embassies. my favourite food is australia, chinese western menu,

lalaine is philippino, australian.thai. The work is done. At makati tienamen bar we signed

at the hieght where 1/2 the work is done, we did the signature for the whole universe. we signed for the world fork and view jamieson valley. we signed for the planet at appartment thailand. we signed in the boards and communities at novatel. the governance for south america continent was signed in the philippines.

the enter were in the philippines. and england, president of france. there were 1 000 limousines of china in the philippines manila for the worlds greatest signature and berth. we were there and saw the

black limousines, consierately the wisdom wall is at the chinese gardens. we went to the chinese gardens rizal park. the work, signature for the worlds workforce WORK

and 0.5 BILLION WORK WAS Signature File at makati hard rock cafe. the defense for england was signed at novatel. settlement in the suburbs is glamourous and like you see so is a kingswood. exclusive was a colour tv.

the hieght of the tree the world in ww2 did response from the radio and also ran the war

from the radio. wikepedia a value to you tells king george won the war. nowadays we have the direction and the immage, the origin is dvd.

the direction is translated in 4 400 languages. we were never away from home with pattaya tv.international channel and not

far thanks to thailand tourist police. our appartment in thailand is our first home since the settlement was stolen in the appartment at bayswater. my first home is bel air. i lived in sydney pattaya bel air 17 years.lalaine and i

have twelwe years and lalaine and philip did the travels together. lucis looked after the office home and mailing destination, good times. The day of attention was the worlds best day and worlds biggest achievement. we lived it for two days

an analogy is the tower seaworld queensland broadwater. 1st june 2019 is the worlds biggest day and we were in it. 2020 is the worlds biggest time. 2000 was a big organisation. 1st june 2020 is the worlds bigest day . there are two in a row.

there were 5 presients in a row. 1/2 the lives are saved and supply economies. we celebrated at centrepoint tower. for vistors we served scones crean and jam, devonshire tea. and ate

prawns or at buffet. for christmas we have seafood buffet

at bayview resturant novatel on beach. these christmas we had christmas platter and friends over at oceanview appartments. after 18 years we sold the gt. we maintained our 3 cars and after 3 years sold the bmw3. we got to each engagement and finished

all of our commitments. we maintained our assetts and made it in 2020. historically the worlds biggest days was when jesus was alive and when and when egypt settled the wars in the other civilisation the vast sucess which the future generations built on the back of.

the three people god spoke to bhuddah lasted forever. jesus king of israel incarnate and son of god incarnate was murdered on a cross and and later risen emmanuel. but when he was murdered israel failed, the worst times not a provident messiah after he was murdered, a bad one. faithfull people written up the times coan bhuddist archive india. Roman helped all the way

and eventually did achieve a resolution for a large number of people after saving thier lives. Joan of arc was burnt at the stake after god spoke to her at 14 at 16 told her what people joan installed and was built the war which couldnt be achieved

the 1st berth of freedom, the built war, won the war and thence in an england main inquest was charged having an evil spirit, talking under her lips, most precious and treasure she is, and joan of arc joan she was burnt at the stake, no one helped.

the biggest work undertaken in the world was the recovery run by constantine and his people constantine people, all rulers like was done today. the passages we 2 years plus 2 years. in the time england scotland went out of tahiti, left the passage

was 6 months, a return passages was 6m 6m 6m 6m return calle d up to 2 years much improvement. something which could have cost you more the you can afford is y2k. now you have seen our history. philip and hays are the youngest in the business. stephen in charge built surrender, at archealogy. hays got a 360 000 000 000 inheritence paid for his work. to run the work i spent 720 000 000 000 in notes. berlin spent 720 000 000 000 in notes. The bhuddist ruler s and breaches and the bhuddist reaches have claim for thier citicens,

RECIEPT 300 000 000 000 000 300 TRILLION. BELIEVE IT OR NOT ARE REAL COSTS. We applaude your grace. in the trade war there are billions of dollars splashing around, if you did banking you can shore, store up some of the billions. I have funders are multi squillions. the people which do the work

in our world are devoted and competent and can do so because the gracefull have some of squillions to draw from and have had to reducing thier personal account. it is suitable

to repair by adjustment where because of event the countries have been cost money. kingdoms are helped out by funders.

i always pay for insurance. i have huge amount of assetts i am called eon and lalaine own.

our assetts at all times are required to run . our personal internal assets are hardworking, we work each asset we own. this could explain if the carpet wears out.

MY OUR STAFF PEOPLE NEW OWNERS STAFF, STUDY STUDY IN THE PHILIPPINES HEAD OF STAFF and new staff SPACE CHARTS have the longest education in the world. we also educate child protection agencies, united nations severe armed forces, which you call seniors and NATO BOUND in

the longest education in the world we built 1982-1984 and started 1986 with compassion existing qualification and education each are expert. Also we do a nuclear rally which is a nuclear education. As boss i was required to get an expert in place at each event around, throughout the world.

This is why i make such a big song about my office built spanning the planet and we keep the office intact. chemical cloride stores of napahm agent orange delderin anthrax was

destroyed and since there has been much progress. Germany is innocent, russia is a major contibutor to the world,

it worked, north korea has been immuculate and so thier friends . there was minimal threat in the world . such environment is a good workplace and could be a lively home. there are many factors influence a home there less factors influence a workplace because of the concord in a world place bringing

you more money in the country making home possible. i also did works like raise morale and reforms wich reduced the number of injuries and deaths from 117 deaths a year to 68 deaths a year and my industry form and broad form an articulation a senior corporate is still survived. the industry was divided and sold, an energy guru and industry boss our sector sold for 1.8 billion dollars to florida light and power i retired senior corpoarate of a 1.8 billion dollar company. i started off the apprentice. i built the 4billion dollars australia transmission works which are sucessfull.

this is the end of

my 2nd career to supply home 1980-2000 i had an affluent home. i moved to sydney 2000. the largest infrastructure spend in australia was 0.5 billion dollars the m7 motorway and m2 link and industrial platform which transformed urban and suburban sydney an d made more money for you.

the largest aligned national

spend is 10 billion dollars infrustructure murray darling basin scheme the two biggest spends in the history of australia

and surrounds . julia gillard was the first woman prime minister and ever remembered. throughout history there have been a substantial number of woman in charge the most powerfull and loving one queen, supply, ally sheba. the world we came into there are a large number of women in charge, in your country you

particually want more women in charge, you have awarded gays leadership and solid leadership of the country a graphic chenge in the world . you will be a new you and new

modells will best suit you and found workin the future. my head retired and i made a speech, i retired i started off the boss in 1991 the work was done by i and my staff, i was paid handsomely. i was the productivity supervisor for 17 countries of the 53 contries commonwaelth.

i built the nuclear retail passages

and was the nuclear retailer supplying uranium and plutonium products to 70 countries to 2014 whence handed over to the new generation. your country and your friends the citiicens whom live on islands and your kingdom have made a fortune more than most people in the world.

\ you have wisely built help in medicare.

my partners have helped me . i was your boss for a long time . the outcomes are most fulfilling. I was in charge of the 6,9 generations of the proffessors and vaulted all the records. Proffessor Bartholemew ran the vaults. You have made a lot of money, Australia is a rich country even though young.

when you conceal god has spoke to you maybee it is an assembly an angel talked to you i councell there are 3 people in history god spoke to and the three people had the biggest results.

2 came to a terrible end.

it is a world which needed cleaning up. the world built to a time of sucess . the time and sucess was documented . both the sucess and the documents is called the 1st catholic. the primary goverment of the world was the first to send the message througout the world and

send

the gift of eternal salvation.

jesus has many names and jesus emanuel has many credential. the name or identity you use is not likely to be recognised in other languages. the do the work the worlds work is

translated in 3 900 languages it has beefed it up helping the world save 2000000000 lives. now all the information is in and i am very clear on your achievements therefore i know what you have done i have written up the whole story, boss to 2014. philip is still your boss as constituents philip and lalaine are

region, region ASIA-PACIFIC REGION. philip is head of secret service, in english retired scientst. In all works england, australia, south africa, canada, CITICEN My Partners Helped. My original Bosses were WRATH, BATH WINDSOR. MY MENTOR WAS DAWN CHAMBERS. I WAS PAID INTO MY BUSINESS. IN Australia I was on and grew in an Australian Paypacket, salary, recreation. I did voluntary works. In INTERNATION And

INTERNATIONAL

My Partners have did, done the work. My first ever boss was Philip GREECE Senior Assasin, World. Philip sent many people in from all over the world to give us an education. My original education was from my birth family. all the work was done to make the writing sucessful.

my 2nd career was to supply home. we had plenty of money.

the settlement for my new house was stolen. the history of the birth family whom are born monies were not completed and to supply home there is a shortfall. i found out

also monies are not completed and settled in another part of the world including to some good friends. this is a better graph to work from. the world and england have been impecable and the biggest results in the history of the world untill event.

I RAN THE SEAT OF INDIA, Me and My Staff for 22 sucessfull years with the 4-6 highest results in the world, the work of my 22000 citicens of england WARD4 Whom are volunteers. My great grandfather was the 1st WARD and had a farm at Lucknow, Orange NSW the built a big business and the father and the mother raised 11 children

supplied by the big business the towns blacksmith industry workshop and retail sales. my grandfather was an accountant had two lives, also an astronomcr. i n the old days everyone

had two lives or had gone to war. my uncle robert came back from ww1 and ww2 and had good service,

my uncle cecil was landbound and won a medal.

the women whom are my ancestors were affluent and had sucessful families. the number of the born family today descended from french nobility the passage of the kingdom os aisles moved to eurpoe is more than 276 children.

the story is written up. Our work is on video library. there is the work of invention lucas hieghts. ASI Library. The standards library is built in wall for engineers to work from by vietnam, World siagon publishing the original store of standards asia pacific region, office. Stunning reasearch in the cosmos . a contrution to reasearch under the oceans, japan professors found anti poles. we healed the generator in fly ships.

in siagon 4 years work. the worlds information

8 000 000 000 people is on dvd thanks to the hard work of the people in the world ethic appointed whom have be in every place all throught the world and sony screens. Administration

is pipes at sanyo hong kong, all together have changed the world in the posotive.

you have done part of the work which changed the world in the posotive. in image and 4 400 languages each nation. tongues with blast. we are working on our rocket and patient with our scientists. we are getting closer.

when you get me, whence we engage you get a lot of people work. my people have retired and now we are less people work, we are 1.300 000 people and staff. the worlds workforce is 0.5 billion people i am 1 of the bosses in charge.

The work in the world is Written. I and my partner own a business. my mother built the fund in 1966. to supply home i have done lifetime of supervision which my father, mother taught me. i studied engineering and business, commerce.

I was a pool salesman which earnt plenty of money. i launched philip kidd space in 1976, built in 1982 and founded international trading plan 1986. I was made boss 1988. I was made Boss, WORLD 1996. Lalaine was born in 15 generations and in supply home won national awards. Cinamen has done world work for all the years and is signature. Charity is region, World Herald.

When the nations did salvage the land we become as won the governors of CRISIS, THE WORLD S NEWEST CONTINENT. WE And THE CITICENS built the NEW SUBURB IN SPACE. More citicens have moved in to Crisis. Philip the Monarch owns and runs the 1ˢᵗ Archepelego. The Governors Mayors

and Citicens Own and Run the 2ⁿᵈ Archipelego. The space workers have worked from the New Suburb in Space, I have too as boss and I have been staff Inter-continental Borders Since

1982. Your world was built from a survey. The constant Survey is on the headland maroubra which is where we go to to go to the wave beach. The Griener family members saw in the building of the rubix cube . space workers drop thier ties to the rubix cube from all over the world when out doing work. the workers in the world work from the geographical, physical location, thank you very much. Flooding in all its dimensions and diagram is run from the production thomas the tank in manila park. we made sure we have been there. we have been to each museum. the new

generations historical museum, world is built in japan. Australia built the collins class submarines in service. the russian submarine has been at ANMM the scotish submarine is at ANMM Perth freemantale I have been to all these places. Built is the Dock new Zealand and greenpeace

rainbow warrier is in museum the boat/ship reef my senior region did captain with survey of the seas sucessfull turned france extension back after the 22nuclear tests france in

the pacific diagram. cinamens father my father built the witch at sea in his command of england navy vessels

, weapons boundary constabulary, which is now the world domain, there has been no more wars.

Mama was murdered at bells pub she owned at 83. i see rory in each year all the way to 2017. Rory still runs the pub. it is the true english style and heaven. the modern world diagram was built from the ensign in bells pub. bells pub has a longest vibrant and affluent history in the southern hemisphere built a long time ago and is a billion dollar real estate. the mansion is 10b and was up to 12b. now 15b. in you selling you are calling a small mansion a mansion

5-6m. sydney mansion has been the most popular real estate purchase. elizabeth retired. the retirement was done for annette, annette went to see uncle kieth and aunty jan. the side of the berth family are the commerce board and kieth and jan oversee with the other members. kieth and jan sold wheat and raised a sucessfull family. annette made a beautifull day with uncle ted aunty gwain uncle ray and aunty sue . ray died of cancer and was a heralded engraver

raised a sucessfull family. uncle ted completed 6 developements the 6 and last japan business lobby

japan sea port, raised a sucessfull family ted and gwain retired in mid mansion at silverdale. the kidd family has one of the largest family tree. we were at cold chisel concert and frontrow at the last concert, nyssa gave me the book working class boy. we have been to concert

guns n roses acdc greenday, i have a song collection 420 cd, INXS. lalaine has a huge movie collection. the plaster linings moulds were brought by an owner whom made business in kingswood i met making all the moulds and building sales . at its origin plaster linings was the only

cornice manufacturer and the products were very popular. uncle bert sold the dodge phoenix and made a quiet retirement. i followed every minute with the friends when canterbury settled in the new clubhouse. our wall was the cantebury wall. we have got a lot of awards. in the world thank yous are made. Samuel milgate rooms were at burwood . the original sydney mansions are still there. later the beaches became so popular a nd later mansions were built by the beach. Golf courses were founded and built and i have played regularly at leonay leura long reef

mona vale little bay i over 38 years. The international surf classic is at narrabeen beach and the iron man at port maquarie sam won the international surf championships when i started out an australian woman. there is many memorabillia. we built up the international

fishing competion brings in 0.5 billion daollars a year for australia equal to the biggest project, my staff built the space and do the switching in each year. my birth family in generations have seen a small country become a great country . and the world built and won a better place.

a further achievement exactly as laid out beyond egypt as founded in jesus days, time, the consquence of AD. the extension the 1st catholic, the return of the wars, the muslim prediction, the muslim extension, the commerce . gods the universal god, plans. we cant do the linear.

we cant see the dark ages, there times are thought to be good and quite peacefull but very few records were kept, we cant see. because there are almost 0 records is because time is called the dark ages.

china did flooding . you can see in the pocket book encyepedia, of the ancient world. an in at archaelogy, and philippines national book store. the new world has separate testables.

the last raid was more the 500 years ago. the most disapointing event in history khmer to great last provider was destroyed and then came the highest rule and god god in earth was

destroyed. the were the people whom surveyed for every king and the king of israel ambient

son of god, god the father whom authourity has gone to the 4 ends of the earth by the very same race of people 15 000 years the king of kings whom each of the race were murdered in 1965-1968 this is the world first intevention and the starting blocks the new world, with a foundation destroyed, our world. there are un - wise in our world

and the world is always working. results bring our planet 8 000 000 000 people into a secure future . population growth, explosion is the result of sucess and population growth should be embraced. len and bet raised a sucessful family. aunty rita lived to 94. philip and pearl the books completed for the whole world and signed of on the telephone . a new generation signed on. ours is automated we have space loggings and space logs stored inside the computers what run the world what jesus only dreamed of and ceasar would have died for built in the 35 years.

aunty leonie aunty janet and philip have the most sucess. our work done on the telephone is in safes, the lower port are the leases to telephone company including

my manual vodaphone. i signed off on the new vodaphone network at waragamba 2 signature and the network mobile network

was up and running the same day a big day and has been profound . joint countries built the new westpac computers and

gay ran the board. the nations installed hotel room saudi arabia. the world citicens were building into the era, what is

built the world citicens depend on and for some of the build you run it. each nation and islands has made a reliable contribution to the world and people live longer.

also the generation in 50 years achieved 50% global warming reductions. malcolm turnbull the thence environmental minister installed our future and our achievement of 50% equal to the achievement of the world generation. Prime

minister julia gillard unvied a future a nd gave each of us a book. john howard wrote to each of us a letter. kevin rudd brought the country to speed. kevin was promoted united nations sectrary general the most sucessfull appointed australian and with your achievement the father of the nation. you paid for the national wall. north korea also built the new processor for the world the americans call the 10 billion dollar chip.

americans paid 10 000 000 000 for each processor chip see time magazine herald. also there is a 50 year pictorial of man landing on the moom. of course the updated

should be man and woman at home on mars. half our people throughout the world are women. when you have moved the obligation of the male australia as the australian

senate has passed order paul model no longer apply. now the processor chip is installed each america agencies are run by the processor chip updated a better solution and working well . the information is on dvd. the highest is paul keating

and paul has done the work for the largest number of citicens in the world, also paul is present prime minister. bob hawke 11 years and john howard 13 years is the longest serving. australian at the top of the world not just bosses from other countries

well done the biggest achievements a profound for are young country there are 6 australians at the top of the world and

also the anglican church has a good reputation. in your country so does the main churches. there we go all have contributed. The main plan. thank you quenten.

thank you governor general the former general. and governor of new zealand. i was boss 1991 to 2014. we love adani. Her majesty has one third power in india and has strength in the

SEAT, Of INDIA. it is all carefully detailed in the movie the blues brothers.

we are most fortunate the war in dia was won. we made it.

I WAS PAID IN 2018. I WAS PAID IN 2019. MY NEW OWNERS HAVE GOT MONEY IN, Lalaine has got money IN, Ratio 460 000.

I WAS APPOINTED AND INSTALLED TO DO THE WEAPONS WORK 2015 FOR THE NATIONS OF THE WORLD, MY STAFF ARE COMPETENT WE WILL DO A GOOD JOB/ WORK. WE WILL EARN AND HAVE AS INCOME 4 000

000 000 000 in the ERA. WE will complete our jobs/work. we face costs due to event.

in 2020 lalaine and i have settled our monies. we have the rest of our lives and look forward to enjoying our time and we have so far. i have installed man.

the saudis are in charge and the complice. For the 8 000 000 000 citicens PRI Is IN CHARGE. For our Region Priority and Priority staff are in charge. i have worked all the years with

my seniors. this is part of the report.

also we contained fukishima power station . i ran the emergency fukishima all the way to completion. scott laid out the papers. i then on the offer installed medics and agreed to

pay for the medics. i wasnt boss when chenoble happened it was before my time but

north korea and relation flooded in to 14 countires in the european boundary which were affected by radiation fallout and kept flooding in for 14 years. in north korea emergency the world has been helping. scott and i saw the alarm. one of the biggest problems we have

is scotland did not alarm weapons, the world couldnot achieve the emergeny but the grace of the peoples of china china did manage to alarm weapons for the world and we cant work out how the people of china maged to achive so much past embrace and past phenomenon and now there is a STAY in the emergency. so far china has saved it. the world is doing 4 more years work tO GO. What we have is fully serviced. lalaine runs our affairs and we have nice reliable competent people in place. Fully managed. at this time the settlement monies is missing.

OUR INTERNAL INVESTIGATION SHOWED THE RULE IS PAID. ALL OTHER NATIONS ARE PAID. The Citicens are Paid.paul. our congratulations to six the wobbly world and five the rickety world, thank you to john kerry, the happenings at the table have been broadcast througouht the word on

national broadcaster. as i have shown you the world was run in the war years from radio. our missions in these years are peace missions. the world is from TV origin DVD a sincere evolution substatial results no diffent to

jesus talked about. of course jesus is called something different in a different language. the work of translation is profound in 4 400 languages the love you put in . to do what jesus, present and john insrtructed means each person in the world gets full benefit= love and also

in 2 you are faithfull to the 1 each. how to love is you have 0 liability. you have love in the part from what you have done but if the strength measures 0 iability you have not impact love in the world and you can rest. gods plan which is hard to build working well in the world

in our times. there are 4 god recorded in the holy bible. one is god of heavens, one is god of heavens, his son whom became flesh. god incarnate whom is god the races in earth whom run the earth, we will call god in earth. the others are rulers. the lower testables are people whom

the rules put in charge . for the roots of your race of people see time team 6. philip was

the missionary for england york division to 12am 20.11.2013 went to all parts of the world,4corners the reticaltion was done by the worlds computer like my wages, england race. holland is innocent ireland is innocent event 2013. such are the christians countries. the

christians have never had more sucess thence in the time of theyre boss.

thank you region1. thank you rule israel. i was born and for a long time we have a palace on lease offered to us 11500 years old and my officials stay there and conduct. your dignities from every nation and reach fly there and do the diplomats and we record the diplomats.

\diplomats are also done in our offices and we record . in our offices lobbys is the diplomatic embassies. i have the diplomatic embassies in place for a global population. also we have hierlooms. lalaine has embassy and hierlooms. lucis has a full testable of vers and more.

lucis built a home office for his firm.lucis is paid . vince is paid vince in 2020 is creditor vince is a best mate does describe the assylum and test and confirm the assylum built is

reliable in information. the worlds most precious jewel is information, the capacity for love.

you love and relay on the holy bible for the information and very wise. the coran india

and bhuddist archive have more information which has gone to the world 4 corners of the world.

you can see it on the nsw state library marble floor maquarie st domain territory world, territory of windsor london. both the bible and the coran is taught in schools in the recent time. i was baptised when i was 6 months old and confirmed when i was 16. i was confirmed with kerry.

i did the appointments with kerry 2 my second. i never did want to not meet with steve and rose the schedule became too full and the money was not paid, stolen. 4 years later the money was not paid, stolen i stopped going to church . i the people and staff could not arrange my

\conducts and affairs with the money stolen and it could not stay in with rose. Rose got a job for 400 000 PA the most pay i have ever seen . your highest income earner is nicole kidman 25 000 000 year. rose was affluent and is your signature. i ran the estate of rose and son.

i and the region staff did james margaret divorce. all is good. john earned 250 000 pa and john earned 400 000 pa. the most money i have ever seen . now all the figures and numbers exist we know ourselves, philip and

lalaine are a 1.6 b client. donald trump is 3.5 billion 3 years including overseas arms. did you know donald trump in the old days from the figures in the apprentice . donal distributed to his wife. donald and his wife distributed to the 4 children. richard branson

made to sam, daughter.

to not include the women name is security, believe it or not. how is your hearing, the radio telescope is fully in touch and with hubble.com images we can see further

to where eternal god lives. at the start of the technology the world chart showed the sun evolved around the earth. when lietenant cook did his journey a scientific mission there was only a map of the northern hemisphere. captain cooks journey is recounted a voyage because from the

foundary our own world will become a planet. all travell was by a sextant. in the bermuda triangle and japan sea compasses spin around because there is an earth gravity, gravametric antipole right through the middle of the earth discovered dimensioned chart and recorded by japan

professors and generators stop producing because there is missing magnetic field we fixed by designing building and installing a blocking pole, yours truly, peter and people staff.

the holy bible exists because some one was faithfull to record. our knowledge of the relationships is enhanced by archaelogy as a ground finding.we wish you the best.

SHEET

SEQUAL
THE DUMB ROAD   VS   COUP CAPITAL OF THE WORLD

SEQUAL _____
IN WORLD'S BIGGEST DAY

_____

1 ST JUNE 2020

_____

1.6.2020
HISTORY
MADE IT IN 2020
MADE IT TO THE END
MADE IT IN 2020   167 000
                                        23 550 000
                                        280 000
                                        500 000 working
                                        500 000 minority investment
                                        438 000 INVESTED

PAID 2018   PAID 2019   4 020 000 000 000
                                        980 000

2022   SALE 205000
                                        SALE 244000

_____
HOUSEHOLD INCOME 2000-2014   1 250 000 PA
HOUSEHOLD INCOME 2014-2022   242 000 PA

_____
PERSONAL INCOME   1990-2000 240 000PA
PERSONAL INCOME   2000-2010 353 000PA
PERSONAL INCOME   2010-2020 755 000PA
PERSONAL INCOME   2020-2022 0   monies stolen

_____

INCOME EXPENDITURE   1, 101, 000
                           360 000 000 000
                           60 000 000 000
                           family 86 000
                           438 000 INVESTED.
                           PAID TO 2022
                           PAID TO 2024
          open   1, 101, 000
                              86 000
          Credit   business loans 14 000
                           medical 16 000
                           developer 8 000
                           Credit 6 000
                           STORAGE
                           DICTATE
                           APPARTMENT BAYSWATER
                           BELT
                           BELT 2
                           THERE ARE 0 OTHER BILLING

CREDITORS   CREDITORS 2000
                           CREDITORS 2000 2020
                           CREDITORS 2000 2020
                           CREDITORS 2000 2020 2022
                           CLAIM
                           CLAIM Vince Parents
                           SALARY
                           2 REGION STAFF
                           @ Office Staff, KEEP RECORDS, Scrutineer.
                           2 charles staff, RACE
                           PRESENT RACE DAY OF ATTENTION, 14
                           35
                           LOSS 34 400 000
                           KINGDOM THEY EQUAL TO RECIEPT
                           RECIEPT 35 000 000 OFFICE HONG KONG
                           TAXATION DUE 2018.
                           THE DEFENSE LAID IN TRIALS IS NOT DUE THE RACE
                              OF PEOPLE
                                AND NOT THUS A RELEVENT CONDUCT RESPONSE
                                IS REQUIRED BY THE BALANCE OF NATIONS>
                           THUS EACH MONIES MUST BE SETTLED

THE INTERNAL INVESTIGATION BY MY STAFF 760 000
2014-2016 2016-2018 SHOWS THE RULE IS PAID.
THEREFORE EACH MONIES ARE PAID, IN EVERY CASE
THE REGION ARE PAID, THE CITICENS ARE PAID
AND THE RELATIONSHIP TO EACH NATION THE
CITICENS ARE PAID. THEREFORE THE HUMAN
CRIME AND HUMAN CONTENT EXIST WITHIN THE
CITICENS
CLOSE

open	1, 101, 000 ! ST JUNE 2020	
	Philip, Lalaine	
	Cinamen 10M	
	Rory 15M	
	COST 19.5M	
	Lalaine cost	0.261M
Balance	1, 101, 000	

DEBTORS
156 000
2 200 000 000
DUE 2026
2025 Senior assasin.
There are over 7 500 000 000 Cases.
1 116 TRIALS COMPLETED

MY OBLIGATION WAS TO HAVE AN EXPERT IN PLACE
THERE IS AN EXPERT IN PLACE BY 2019
AT THE TIME I HAD AND AN EXPERT SEATED AND EACH PERSON IN THE
WORLD
PERFORMANCE AND WAS THE BIGGEST ACHIEVEMENT IN THE HISTORY OF
THE WORLD.
THE WORLD LIVED THE BIGGEST ACHIEVEMENT IN 16 500 000 000 YEARS 2 DAYS.
LEAD, BOSS
THERE WAS PERFORMANCE BEFORE 10AM.
THE WORLD HAS SINCE ENCOUNTERED THE 14 RACES Of 27 000 RACES.
EACH BUSINESS IS IN PROFFIT AND WORLDWIDE LALAINE AND PHILIP MADE
8470 PROFFIT IN THE ENTIRE EMPIRE, Office of Dignity

and EACH CHARGE 1 300 000 PEOPLE AND STAFF AND RAISED 23 550 000.
PHILIP AND CINAMEN MADE 28 000 000.
THE TOTAL MONEY INTO OUR BANK ACCOUNT IN DISTRIBUTABLE CURRENCY
IS 1, 596, 856, 725 CELEBRATING 40 YEARS.
THERE IS AN EXPERT IN PLACE I HAVE MET MY DUTY AND ORDERLY
AS A BOSS OF THE WORLD AND FINISHED THE WORK MEETING MY OBLIGATION
AND FINALISED MY DUTY. LALAINE AND I WORKED THROUGH EACH DECISION
AND LALAINE AND I DID THE SOLVING, WE GOT THE WORK RIGHT.
WE RETIRED IN 2020.
IN DEDICATION TO CINAMEN AND CHARITY WHOM LAID THE TRIEN.
I WAS BORN AND DID THE SIGNATURE, WE HAVE SIGNED SEALED AND
DELIVERED A WHOLE PLANET AND SIGNED EACH BERTH OF ONE LOVE.
IN MAKATI WE SIGNED FOR THE UNIVERSE. WE DID EACH ENGAGEMENT
AND EACH APPOINTMENT IN PERSON.
SEE YOU ABOARD THE FLEET.
WE ARE THE WESTERN WORLD PETRA FLY CHARTER ABOARD PHOENIX.
EACH OF OUR PERSON IS CONSTITUENT ASIA PACIFIC REGION.
Philip and Lalaine Are Region and region, ROCKETMAN.
Philip is senior assasin, Head of secret service.
CITICEN, EMPLOYER, PARTNER, FAMILY MEMBER, MEMBER,
BOSS OF THE WORLD 1996,2002, BLUE.
Lalaine is Born, Boss. Boss member of commerce board
born in 15 generations, head of family. head of study.
boss. employer. boss. lalaine runs philip and lalaine affairs.
we sign for 2 240 000 000 people. the north korea rocket
science factory is the consumate korea is the largest
institution in the world and the members sucessfully serve
over 5, 600, 000, 000 citicens in the world has made our
world a better place. the members of south korea are deployed
permanently in north korea with familys. the members of
south korea are deployed permanantly in south korea
with familys because of the wall barbed wire.
my office is in north korea. my office is at hong kong
we are sea and seaboard. our berth is emerald palace
china domain wall 1990. I have jurasdiction in
240, 39, 191 countries we have an office in each
country, london hall and vaults united states of america
berth, and our service registration is
ANSTERDAM INTERNATIONAL AID ADMINISTRATION we run from the
MAGNOLIA HONG KONG AND ARE ORDERED BY IMMUNION TOWERS.
In emergency we used the aerial board HUMMERS.
MY STAFF ARE ORDERED BY THE CONSUMATE OUTCOME OF THE

NATIONS OF THE WORLD as installed from supply to bosses
or as intervened by the world DEFENDER.
philip and lalaine are 1%.
philip is boss 1996 promoted. We have C.V.
My organisation is fully serviced, in a right
relationship we owners are, founder. In a wrong
relationship i continue to act, In 2015 I
was instructed to build an assett register 2018
by the world commerce, bosses, nations and have built
an assetts register 2018. the scheduled assets are
listed at charles massih + co,amber, lalaine.
In 2015 i was appointed and installed to do the
WEAPONS WORK 2015 for the nations of the world.
I and my staff run the building of the borders
africa continent and is sucessfull. I am staff since 1982.
Lalaine is staff since 2008. Sucessfull. for the
8 000 000 000 citicens there has been donation, lease
palace, london hall, land for vaults, porting done.
In event(negative) i paid 30 000 000 000AUD for
additional passage and answered INQUEST.not our fault.
12.5.2020 jay and julie flies to korea.
The 2nd work is to feed 20 billion people.
So many people have been encouraged to do what it is
to change the world and so many people have done
and so many people worked hard in the worlds plans and
ultimately there is sucess. it is one of my duty as dignity
to record work done and there are sufficient records.
It is also our job to research, there is 0 decision the WORLD
made responding to event which is not right there is 0
capacity for the offense or the identified. the account
has been laid and the secure investigation is complteted,
in outcomes. the secure investigtion is the investigation
by 30 installed countries on behalf of all countries
30 installed in the WORLD 16 years of planning.
the records are reply generation computers and human
courts records, solving laid geneva and handsard.
a lot of things we done is in case the world gets there
but when the world achieves the level of organisation
the world because of preparation is booming on. i have
done the signature and we are the first to be there,
other people will follow doing work, world and our planet
in the future can potentially be a better place like our

time the world is a vastly better place. at the same time
the work done in our planet is sealed. like in the holy
bible times testables are built and chronicles are built.
these report are part of the worlds testables and are due
to be laid. history is formed over 60 years. a government
builds 30 years into the future, the world builds 300
years into the future how we achieve to serve every person.
i am an eon built since 1982. my rational is 10 power 2.
we have the highest results in the world.
every nation in the world has made a significant and major
contribution over the 75 years. the people whom live
on islands are union of nations and have made a major
contribution, in the asia pacific region one third of the
constituents live on islands far more people than the rest
of the world live on islands and enjoy. the islands now
have an emergency shelter and when there has been a problem
is supported by flooding. we had on event fukishima
power station a deterioration was contained a part of the
worlds flooding effort and people came from every country
to work, i the region ran it and in 2014 supply medics.
scot laid all the plans out and the experts came in
to work from the plans. proffessors lead calculation.
the concrete pump was supply from florida to repair the
crack in the bough caused by earthquake. two electricians
gave thier life to repair the damaged cables in the
bough, basement essential to the plant operation, i councelled
the two electricians, the people were evacuated.
fukishima runs today with one chamber down and
nuclear energy contributes the consumate of global
warming reductions. for the british emppire i was
the nuclaer retailer for many years and sold
uranium and plutonium products and supply and waste dump
to 70 countries 22 years of sucess and i was paid
940 000 000 philip and cinamen,
we invested the 940 000 000 in our
organisations and ulitimately increased the number
of staff, my staff have big surprise, all the time
i have been building staff, my staff have been
building offices. our personal income was 755 000pa
plus each account business operating monies.
monies were stolen and cinamen is a creditor.
we had a good 20 years and a whole lot of life and

the most wonderfull friends, we loved our staff and
our staff are fulfilling we grew our income and assetts
and worked to supply home. we effectively ran our assetts,
and the girls built the girls effort, assetts and the girls
laid the trien, we wanted more time together and
instead we got less, we completed but the plan
didnt pay off, niether one of us had an amount of
complaint for each other and there was 0 divorce,
we loved our years and our times out the dance and
dinner with friends and our activities and we were
famous and i found out later we still got fans of our walk.
my chair and office are built nowadays we have it all
at our fingertips. i moved into the office when the settlement
monies were stolen and we live in the office a fringe benefit.
our new home was in pattaya. i married a second time and we much
enjoyed our years and have substantial growth
and lalaine and philip have effectively ran our assetts
and we did the travels and each engagement and appointment.
in each effect there is a diplomatic embassy. god bless.
we have have had a ball of a time. my both married
family are the most good people and my both married
family i love . lalaine gives the good parents
a middle class retirement. collette is my half wife.
peace and i have authour. destiny and pri are in
charge. rose my girfriend we didnt make it further
when the monies was stolen the work to move my
affairs wasnt achieved, this is the first harm
from monies stolen, in march 2013 the staff wages
were not paid and a full ambient investigation
was begun by the world and nations of the
world using the information in the world computers.
the world is continually doing work which observes
the offender, after event 2013 the world is doing
work which obeys against the offender and later
the worlds computers running are calculating
against the offender despite all this there
is no response from the offender the same as
the offender history, incredible. you can
see the history in wikepedia. the ordeal
which works is the ordeal of the offender BOSS.
We had premium results untill the time. 5 500
Precious lives were shed on borders at the

will and installation of the offense.
the race won the most huge claim in the
history of the world the records from dark ages
the first picture of how bad the offense is.
because of the offense the inputs are not done.
my business partner retired and elizabeth retired.
philip has funders. my friends remain.
as owner i have had the same employer 26 years.
huge complaints were made about jesus as you read
the recorded in the holy bible in the same jesus
drinks and smokes and lends his arse to other blokes
by unreliable, bad people but as for you never make an
illicit complaint against anyone. you can make
the biggest difference in the world by being good
in your suburb. we have been working on function
in my assetts. the sanhedren made the complaint jesus
has torn the race down and jesus was murdered, forfiet
but make sure your work is right. but at the end
the offender wont correct, the offender just ofends,
tells lies and filthy jokes.ben alias saw to it
but ben did copt the preservation. estaban is training
to be a pastor and will soon have it resolved. this
is what happened since your work pastorIIIX the
pastor whom has 8 mistresses paid for by the church.
the balance of nations didnt recognise the union
of aggressorIIIX but King HENRYIIIX is a solid case.
so is the case of sheep and the good sheppard.
it couldnt have happened without joan of arc
or napolean.most of you know this man as a singer
but there is a whole lot more like maddonna.
elton john the most senior, demonstrable lord will
do the marco polo for england around the world.
england 140 countries scientific mission is the
mission to south pole 114 ships. england last scientific INVENTION-good
mission is led and command by lietenant james cook. if
sucessfull england will make a fortune as much as
putting man on the moon for each country, i sold
uranium and plutonium products and made a fortune for
the kingdom and i and cinamen was paid handsomely,
a peacefull way to win the war built over 14 years.
the close of 1,116 trials the ground built from
the record installed by dawn delay host and concern vince. vince

70

and vince parents has the biggest claim aligned
and laid by the secret service and an evacuation
identified because of illicet complaint, called irregular.
so far 0 claims are paid 0 compensations due are paid.
the rulers have accounted at hotel room saudi arabia 2017. Same as history
when rose got a job paying 400 000pa moved to queensland
and john was paid 250 000pa and john 400 000pa some of
the berths in the country affluent now would be 600 000pa.
only a fool wouldnt move with rose and only a fool would
give away cinamen, try to stay awake, see singer
passenger song, dont let her go. for the story of sarah
sam and melissa see paul kelly song, to her door and
to see australia in colour see artist darcy doyle and a
kingswood brochure and try to ignore the petrol prices.
the asia pacific region tanker deliver to you now she
is built by samsung shipyards and the price of petrol
in your country is 22 cents per litre cheaper at the
bowser, the impact to make your country great, strength
for your business and savings for the government thank you
generations of the asia pacific region family,
our love for the family, our love is a light.
in the corona virus the petrol price has fallen to 90c/litre
The only rely required from us is our household income.
quatar was indebted and this is highly irregular.
quatar is at emergency desk.
the only rely required is our household income has
happened 2 times. us, iran is bomb air base 0 casualty.
USA to port out of Hawaii.
the only rely or artifact required from us is our
household income. doctor of ives ally the demonstrable
and immediate princess china the competent power.
it is a better world. the biggest results in the world
and the biggest results in the history of the
kingdom of england, 141 countries.
solidarity european, 121 countries all in.
governance south america continent all in. russia relation all in.
africa continent borders are being built.
philip and peace is the former head of
united nations armed forces salary whom are
in charge of the armed forces and service
from each nation whence in territorial land
or service.philip is the head, secret service

and served many years . philip does figures.
philip is also grace labor party global.
the missions are sucessfull 0 dead.
my organisation is sucessfull 0 accidents.
PRI IS IN CHARGE.
for the developer PARIS is in charge, paris hall in usa.
for energy 8 000 000 000 people mr arnold swartzeneger
has vaulted the information in vault, california to hall.
mr arnold swartzeneger is also the governor of california
and is his hall. mr swarteneger is also famous actor.
IN THE ASIA PACIFIC REGION PRIORITY IS IN CHARGE.
THE HEAD OFFICE IS IN JAPAN.
THE RECORD IS, NEW GENERATION THANK YOU
AND RECORD OF VAULTS, INDIA PROSECUTING.
SAUDI ARABIA DOING THE VICTIMS CASE.
THE WORK HAS BEEN PERFECT SO SAYS MR SENSIBLE.
brought to you by Mr and Mr Asia. I ended
23 years of yacht races and yacht racing first
working for ben lexcen, engineer. philip
was my first ever boss, dawn chambers was my mentor.
philip and eve and even have chartered. i have
passaged billions of people i have done pathways
all my adult life. annette did
not want to and there was a converse in 2004.
annette is a sucessfull mother and there is
writing the wedding of nyssa and brodie a
consumate wedding and a beautifull location
and uniquely and outdoor wedding.
the event engagement was in peru, piccu machu.
work was done for annette.drew is innocent
and does rely the statute kingdom of aisles.
annettes retirement
was done by the world work in 2014 2015.
the world has producing closed nato borders in 2014.
in march 2013 the world compound members was not paid.
in 2016 the settlement of boundaries was done.
once again the world is a better place.
the world 8 000 000 000 citicens get into a secure
future by results. the results verify your good work
love devotion and grace and relevent ambition.
we are proud to be part of good outcomes.

SHEET

Ihave a number in each box now
the boxes for the race were not done
i wanted to see the race claim producing.
all other works is attended. in a 2nd time
the biggest achievement in the world,
congratulations. most people have security.
we are having the balance of the work done.
the workload can now be adjusted.takes 2 years
will be done by the new generation. we
abide with our friends 2020.
the world has saved 2 000 000 000 lives
and on the way to saving 3 000 000 000 lives.
philip has 16 retirement and released of
service 2016. my people have retired and
my people are a new generation.
in join we are 1 300 000 people plus friends.
aunty leonie is the last survivor and has the
best results in the world and we have the best
results in the world also we have sucess.
the work was done at the dining room table
and is in safe.,
memory. the reason why the work is in safe
is the work can be played back again and again
and the worked is installed right, the work
is played back and there is no mistakes in
the installing the work and this is what is
done by the worlds work. the world
has a more competent agility using the
new generation of computer. the original
computer was vaccuum computer before
computer was launched in to the boundary
above 44000 mile in our solar system.
one of the vast advantage of having the
computer in the boundry above 44000mile
is none can go there to mess it up
like happened on the day and you
dont get the worlds biggest mess.

it wont happen in november 2020
because the world wont seat england again,
and also the enforcements begun
assure what happened and the horror wont
happen again and there will be no pain
nearer to revelation. by doing such
actions the world has already wiped
the tears away from every eye like
the kmer doand as the kmer do
so equate the biggest mess in
the modern history of the world.
. god speed to you.
when philip, greece was senior
assasin the boss of the world bad
people used to jump the walls,
today we might get through in the
old days and jesus days they had
not only problems to deal
with and get a result but also
predators lively and deadly animals
and was half the work what a huge challenge.
alltogether the work has cost
us >220 000 000 000 the
monies stolen is >10 200 000
in this unique case you can
find out what is done before the
history books are form because
the actions are equal to what is done
found by the secure investigation.
so for the first time what is done
because of secure investigation
is known by the whole world,
unique achievement. i am
a primary investigator of
the nuclear world but this
is not a component of
investigation
this is a
part history.
SHEET
REPORT

now we have found it all hinge on the secure investigation
is how the world is getting to result, now what does it all
swingfrom, i have written up the nations story, this is
one of my obigation as boss and the supply has come
from each nation and there has been many people do the
work, it is my obligation to align the supply and
deploy as i have done and you see here. i have done
much work in my ambition to be a good boss and i have
been a boss 75% of my adult work and now it is the
information does add up i am a good boss and we are
ready to go again. lalaine is also a good boss.
all i have to do is find the information at the
time the information is to be laid and thats the balance
of the work. sarah is the region funder and constance
is the region material funder . each citicen is defended
by a nuclear relay built and include you.
this is the end of my work and obligation the balance is
it now exist in written and can be found if the store
is carefull and can be distributed. thus instructions are met.
thank you for your help.
all my work as an owner or dignity must be in handwriting and it is.
the work is made and distributed. as a result of the hold there is
0 nuclear threat, the problem is in ground weapons.
the world so far has done 50% of the work and it remains the
biggest mess in modern history. you are half way to securing.
this is where i signoff because philip and lalaine are
retired in 2020 our 20 th retirement. i have done
2 lifetime of service and had 2 careers and done space
since 1976. all the work paid off and the writing is
sucessfull. i am a sucessfull commercial - writer.
i do work for the world and for us we have the rest
of our lives. i give you our hottest tip, space is
what assetts the 45 000 kingdoms of the world own,
the volume of the 8 000 000 000 citicens,
if you were thinking of something else you were
thinking of space missions. i cut my teeth as
i ran the original ulysees. the fleet, submarines
and people were the descendents of the worlds
first ulysees, built by my uncle cecil. uncle
cecil was awarded the highest medal. in
australia surrounds tom uren and angus heuston
were awrded the highest medal, the former

governor general of 20 years was awarded the
highest service. we have a black range rover
which has finished duty and the people whom
are the boss respondent. i had a minder.
in 1990 a limousine was commisioned. we had
everything and my study and study completed
i have enough money and i have plenty of money
.i am paid for my work and this work and we were
PAID 2018
PAID 2019
The organisations are paid to 2024
philip and lalaine is paid to 2022.
I am a bachelor of arms, warrant and writt.
I also hold all the 18 nuclear licences
We also have the developement licence
and i am an energy expert and
licence space physcics
and do do work on nuclear power stations as well
as weapons work and energy work.
I am a doctor of arms and we chart as the doctor service worldwide.
you can read our story in life story 1 and life story 2.
lalaine and i have had a large amount of money stolen and i am
looking for additional work. the monies stolen is for
dictate distribtion creditors and our retirement monies.
each transit from my bank account to my australian business
bank account has been stolen and my personal account was stolen.
i have earned the money 2 and a half times and every $1 is stolen.
for 19 years we have faced a bad offender and when i am 60 i want
more relaxation and lalaine wants some peace the race wants to get out
and the rest of the world wants a resolution but a small amount
of your grace will do me 400pw. as a response our organisation
has no job under 3b we are paid 80b pa to run the building of
borders africa coninent and there is sufficient money in 4500
accounts and 8 accounts and 4 accounts php and thb and
insufficient money in 38 accounts the australian business component
the balance 23 550 000 and sufficient money in main account and hk1
and sufficient banking and the doel munns have sufficient banking,
we look to pay for home1 and home2 and office of dignity and
store 1 600pw. all the business costs and bills and cars are
paid to 2022. in case you missed it 1600 pw out of
4 020 000 000 000 in the era is a clear identity of the offender.
dont worry the work is accurate we have had and idenity of the

offender all along and cant go wrong even before you got to it.
its good to to have have one up your sleeve and i wish you all the best.
the worlds got gold out of tracing the money, clear identities and number,
it takes years to trace the weapons and is the bulk of the work.
lalaine has the biggest sucess, lalaine is a member of commerce board
born in 15 generations and the commerce board the generations in the
philippines fourth the world have been in charge of the endurance
of ally 3 and 100% of ally3 are home. the prelude is general
macarthur win and lalaine took me to general macarthur statue
and the general macarthur burial site all the figures are there
and the information is laid as well as a commemorative memorial.
we have been to each museum in philippines and thailand.
all written up now it is like having a museum of you own.
leura was affluent, own you own paradise and the appartment was affluent.
we have spent 10 years by the sea everything we have got has
an ocean view and i never get tired of the ocean view and
lalaine loves the sea, ocean view, in 2008 we decided by the sea.
we had an affluent life now we have a luxury life with lucis in
share with us . our home has members whom are nice. and now you
have enough information to find your way around and for the expert
also calculate the arms formations in the world the work of people
whom love keep you alive and you have more babies our dependency on food.
the depiction is the harvest.

actions 2014 by joint nations
all the rest of work is secure defense for england.
philip and lucis installed sign the defense for england york scotland.
the papers came to me the dignity after the surrender was signed.
there is no other work done. projects are not being completed
because of the demand of the world work a partial slow in the world.
the world and worlds people have 4 more years work to go.
the world is the most grace you will have, the world means
the 8 000 000 000 people populations. the assetts named WORLD
belong to the 8 000 000 000 peoples or union which means the bosses
like myself and lalaine or the inter-nation assetts and the world
assetts including the world computers and the property of the
generations of the world the 2 system in the world by which the
world is run and is sucessfull. dont be too confused england call
everything in the world a system in thier language and retail
and probably in your language if you are a buyer. there are
2 systems. the balance of running the world and your
communities is called commerce and the central is the harvest.

what runs australia, surrounds is called the westminster hall.
the pharoah is the one whom will take the glide up to heaven
and every kingdom has a pharoah and a passage is the citicens.
never want to go to heaven early and never give up your life,
love on another, the girls are owners of an embargo and part
own expansion the hard rock cafe and have demonstrated as have been
done in the past and when the commitment christianity which
means the citicens in christians countries are looking
abroad love one serve all/
we signed at the hard rock cafe at makati and the emblem
is a memmorabilia authentica, elton john it is worth fortunes
probably more than michael jacksons underpants which was
the biggest price achieved at auction cruising up there
with the holy grail. which leaves me not
much to say, what can i say, well done.
you are more than impressive. boss.

THE PUPOSE OF THIS BOOK

*to identify the work done clearly

the propriety of the work done

is 8 000 000 000 at the world record.

the citicens is installed in generation form computers

*for adults growing up in all ranks so you can find your way around. to
a thank you

FOI

* part of the world testables

LAY UNITED NATIONS NEW GENERATION OFFICE,
BANKOK Demonstrates the world is forever building.

what the world do is what jesus instructed after
2000 years is substantially evolved. the 1st record
is the descendents of bhudah. bhuddah laid 500 years before jesus, The
propriety of the heritage of the world and the bosses

of the world, there are 220 bosses, world magistrate, world coroner and
4 world congress, countries are supplied from the world table.
the first record of jesus was recorded by bhuddah descendents and is
till prominent today.

if you are a great achiever you can be the representative of your country
at the world table. if you are nice person you can divide and maybee make it to
the prime minister or mayor. it is all there on alex hood cd. if you want an
adventure you can be a drover. it is all there on alex hood cd. if you have a
time machine you can go to lebanon which in the holy bible is described as
a land flowing with milk and honey!, Yahoo!. For our world
the worlds conduct is on dvd. we have milk the country is full of cows,
for the capacity to run a democracy country it is important each person watches
produce, the ww2 was run from the radio. it is the essential education for
your response. advertisment for democracy countries or dont expect you ruler to
run the country sucessfully. thank god you did allright so far. for 6 years
russia is a democracy and going profoundly well. russia is huge contributor
to world peace. peace in our time is low crime. the world ever works
towards a material peace and i have with my people supply for 27 years.
philip and hays, world normal is the youngest in the business. we started at 22.
Hays and people built and run the world bank the longest group of computers
in the world. we expect your needs will be serviced. member.
\the next generation is AI and ultimately i will be replaced by a shiny machine.
we thank you for the work with you, the world is a better place for your prescence.
copywright house of coconut and wood.
THE WORLD COMPOUND

The Dirty dozen the men whom changed the shape of ww2
if you want something from australia mr malcolms
dirty dozen women will give your country a fresh look.
Australia is a country of the british empire.
There is not only a liberation for gays there
is a good conciousness for women. almost no
homosexuals exist nowadays and the ones condemned
2000 years ago were gerth offenders, liars do exist
and are serious or severe or bad offenders and wont
see the kingdom of god mr alias, liars were the gerth
of some of the bad deeds and at the seat of the worlds need
to respond. i have done work for the world for 30 years
and my work is accurate, reliable. in the history of england

gays was not allowed because the kingdom of england was
hellbent on maximum population growth for theyre
excursions and this is how it happened a verse on england
not a determination or consideration of gays but a avenue
to more babies and the rules and laws a means to more
babies now not wanted for many years because the economy
can support, mr ben alias. and this is how it was when
australia was settled probably as paperwork in london
and when the first colony arrived which was in 12
ships. before gays were allowed and
before gays were forbidden, in the holy bible days hygene
was a consideration and practice forbidden. many people
do do such practices in the west long term in the
gay and straight comunity and also cavity search,
hopefully a quality technology is used are
community standards, accepted. it is different
in some of the world whom are conservative. it is
not right to be a liberal country and rule out all
the citicens whom are liberal. the apply is 2000 years ago,
you are right it is as the bible reads, most likely gays
will go to heaven but malpractice disfunction and
severity will not see the kingdom of god and i would
read the malpractice malfunction and severity will
not go to heaven, ben, the people whom surveyed,
my constituents and the witness and my rely to reporters.
it is done 2000 years ago when there is limited ability
with hygene and containment, these are not only
modern countries but sophisticated countries with
handles on hygene and stringent controls and so
were the ships.the kingdom give theyre citicens a better deal.
as you can see the decree was a bad deal for gays at the time
and a big deal for babies whom mature in the cause and a
degeneration for those not in the cause is the consequence
of the other decrees and the human contact with aboriginal
is the remaining concern, now addressed, the kingdom has
such right with the citicens to 70 years ago. at no time
should an adult enter by any mean a child. not a child
and adult in keep in some other countries is 14 or 16
and not 18 in most countries and this is reliable.
such person whom take a younger wife are betrothed and
wed colloquially called arranged marriage.
in jesus days not a child and an adult in keep was 14.

holy mother mary was 14 when god chose. if you want a sponsor,
i can tell you gay isnt as likely to serve you, dont be foggy,
get out of it. but as for countries it is not your country,
when in rome do as the romans do, in no case wherever in
the world is the practice less than jesus instructed
and almost always more with more entitlement and consumative right.
the highest aim achieved is no crime beyond revelation by taiwan and japan.
we consider each good country. and is there a downturn
in country music we as a nation should adrress and change
the constitution if necessary, and this was the constitution
and the good man would take the woman as is done in some countries
today, therefore 14. keep means the man is providing and
supplies an enviroment the minimum of his duties. in your
country australia you have distribted some of the resposibilities
of the male or senior to women and the paul model does not
now apply to you, the model is the responsibilities and the age is 14.
some things do go astray. the paul model no longer apply to you.
do not apply teach or preach or build from the model dominion paul
the offender saul a murderer. for your kingdom is built from
st pauls cathedral where the cieling is painted by michael angelo
and for other orders kingdoms and countries is built from at time
after and built from somewhere else i have recorded and available
as a search not built from st pauls or the time or the datum
later named st pauls cisteen chapel, god bless. slim dusty
is a good creedo i love to have a beer with duncan because
ducan is my mate and i live near the hotel where slim dusty
wrote the song one night staying in the hotel slim dusty
sold the most cd albums in australia. and had 80 albums.
the monaro is now built in england. life was just like you see in the
old tv series and show and a kinswood was just famous.
my parents drove a kingswood and an upper model and i drove a kinswood
and an upper model and did 1 400 000 km in australia in a gt 700 000 km
my private car and 700 000 km in cars and trucks owned by someone else.
we have a spyder and a gt and a bmw3 3 cars and i kept my last gt for 18 years and had 2 cars.
australia and america was built around the motor vehicle and drive in movie was popular. i did over
30 years of engagements and appointments and stayed in a motel, resort.
as i have shown you in tradition the man paid, the woman run the home and it is the woman as an
outcome had authority as is paul model and much loved and the countries
were prosperous but for this country because of rules made is now in the past, this does not put such
abide in other countries in the past and you should not intend to.

country music is probably an education, i can tell you rock music is an education and maddonna is a separate classroom and john paul gives the certificates, pop music is an education. i used to be told god knows some people love you but i dont and then id eventually grow up.
philip kidd boss

philip and staff and 22000 volunteer ran the seat of india ward 4 from 1991 to 2014 and the developement of australia new caledonia, solomons, samoa now developed - STATEMENTS. before philip and staff 1991 my father and 22000 volunteer.before my father my grandfatger, before my grandfather my great grandfather the first ward, seat of india in charge of the
6 countries and lived with his wife in private berth, her majesty elizabeth II has
one third power in india. the world is changed and vastly better when the wars in india are won. god pity ghandi and elate him in heaven and martin luther king and mandella the consumate of the citicens.
the bosses of the world today live in private berth, the appointments of rich kingdoms run castle. in war the aim is to take over castle.like an indiana jones movie, your best guide to our world. it looks good and the weapons done are a good hold into the future, things can go wrong in our world and have done in the past, hopefully nothing goes wrong and the weapons done are a good hold
into the future. i commend you are nice people. Such is a full diagnosis and prognosis. dialysis is laid.

ALL REGISTRIES GO TO OFFICE

Dear ben alias and solomomn islands, the offender is found in malparctice with weapons and the offender is found in disfunction immediate, the abhorance is found in abhorance immediate and the berth is malfunction by all means available, the identity of the abhorance is the same as the identity of the berth and there was commenced a global man-hunt, this is clear evidence of a aggressor. the history is coming up to war, the settlement the faulklands war,
and coming out of the gulf war, the settlement 2 times the number of people dead.
the history was good and 14 years 0=dead and has happened between 2013 and 2018 and continues is the defense for the offender. quite a number of times gays have continued to approach me and consequitive times even though i have been clear, and there must be an end,
if agaapproaches you it is not a consequence and be as polite as you can if you have been clear and it is a number of times and consequitive you are heading towards the need for an end. i was straight and unwavering and for 46 years, i married at spec the third sex at 46 and
47
after completing 2 unions and am the 3 rd sex after 46 we dont have a full practice ot sex so we still get what we desire and has been wonderfull but the being no boy in you, being identified girl at 14 and 16 and all the time and having no boy in you is genuine, and in 1969 resolved an female, the third sex, the opposite equation is a tom boy these are nice people. a boy being a girl is drag and we dont like it and we dont accept and is gay, to be a genuine the third sex is not gay but a genuine travel in gay, pure. i was straight and straight thinking honourable and reliable and in both times

even married to a genuine i am not gay and dont like gay and wouldnt want gay and couldnt stand gay what i like. it is important for someone gay to like gay and a child at school is at no time gay and when gay is demonstrate and the person is over 16 or 18 demonstrating the you conclude the person is gay and at no time conclude a child is gay . elton john swerved and of course there is a whole world of difference the world of gay elton john in england

is your boss being the most, demonstrable lord, from 1991-2014 i was elton john boss,

elizabeth II was our boss and we are official. elton john will do the marco polo around the world a genuine world leader, mine is love. gay is a man and man or

a man and woman and only those people whom are in charge are man, the person not in charge are not man and have to be very high up to be men and while this is true today it is also how it was in the holy bible times and jesus times and

50% of times the one in charge is a woman. the commoner in no case is man or men unless installed this is very hard to work out. the relation and constiuents accepted lalaine a genuine as the region apply 2008 acceptance and installation 2010 a consumate year and for me a loving devoted and genuine and competent partner,

and lalaine born in 15 generations a competent ruler.

thank you for your grace you have been loving and friends, i have done both but not all 3 and that is plenty of clear battlelines between you and gay, dont invent an unecessary ordeal. if you do what is unessecsary there is unlikely to

be defense for you and you have not honoured you straight love one or have not payed the or stayed on the path and this is relationship. to stay on the straight path is about

conduct and means to stay on the straight path you do no crime and in the case of our

countrys you pay your taxes. i hope its not too big a volume. a relationship is enjoyable the load is to hold down a job/work. every male wants to be called a man and ordered as a man

and every female wants to be called a woman and ordered as a woman. this our world not the old world.

every genuine wants to have friends and love. annette supplied home for taylor a genuine and loved is where i got the thoughts from. it is most auspicious we are thinking of each other. the country is the highest taxed country in the world and is the liberal turnbull constituton mandate in the election and this is where you could do work . there must be means for smoking.

there is 0 convincement, everything was running perfecty in 2013 and here is your bible and here is your scroll. remember to pack a lunch, see kerry packer book, lunch. as a moving in present

to

our home at antipolo in the philippines our nieghbours gave my partner mrs margaret packers book. margaret packers flower arrangemnts which we teasure. It has taken 20 years to put it all together, 20 years and 20 years and now we are celebrating 40 years. i began as the ASIA - PACIFIC REGION, TECHNICAL IN 1980 and built the 2nd side of the world SECURITY.

Charles was the TECHNICAL and built the first side of the world SECURITY. I have met each of the 3500 born to it and a third of the new generation just over 7500 born to it and rehearsed with each world leader and made for each world leader. we did signature for you and your future generations, we kept file, and am known as the worlds no1 negotiator, the bosses brought you revalation and the new world and lalaine born

and grandfather brought you each member of the armed forces home intact, and the bosses built
and installed the governance of south america continent a whole world

and i am delighted to

meet someone born to it, we wish you peace. when the fukishima power station went through earth quake

and was on fire the telephone rang to me the boss within 2 hours and everyone was at attention, i was 2 months on the telephone and with my other duties i was on the tephone half the day, my boss got cranky.

you have a reckoning with you, jesus was born to it

but uniquely jesus was the son of god the father. god the father reckoned with bhuddah and mahomed and and era not recorded in india and the message is in our four corners our world

and above thebes and the bhuddah prefects, and made with people in the mountains and with people in tibet

laos rivers which means above bangladesh, and the holy mother was visible and seen above mountain in

2000 by a large witness and some of the testimony was at roman, st marys cathedral, land, soil australia

sincere berth sydney, know as stmarys cathedral in 2000. a commercial is head and the stations of the cross

bangladesh was the delta and developed by the kmer and people.

the kmer developed all the agriculture and agriculture in all india, the world is developed in agriculture

today the agriculture we depend on the foundry of our economy and the agriculture to feed
20 billion people.

agriculture is the science and technology of the kmer, kmer people.

as a developer i and my people, persons are named after, kmer = celestial and angkor wat was, is the celestial

city, the kmer and the kmer and people and the consumate kmer people are celestial and the celestial people.

elizabeth as a developer is celeste and we are THE ASTORIA WALL. The world built for you
PETERS WALL, MADRID

the leader of tibet is the worlds most secure leader, the ruler in israel the same people as the prime minister of israel long serving is the most, thence the demonstration china and china south america

and the ruler and president mr putin people which has brought you the most concious world in the history of our universe and we and we berlin and host are preceeding boss, the longest rule in the world

now is saudi arabia, relation and then egypt and the central space station 8 000 000 000 people
a world revelation, the confidence built by the 1st generation, we are the 2nd generation petra,
finished we are petra 2, named after petra is in jordan, gods people in the holy bible one of the
twelve tribes of judah see indiana jones epic which makes it understandable in an present language,
our tribulation is the indiana jones theme, my people and citicens are the world surveyor the walk

84

of life and in charge are pa and pa the most senior rulers. we traditionally have done both works and the consumate work and the world, philip also developed the long mental health board and have awards, medals

the long mental health board and service and services for the 120 solidarity the 120 nations armed forces

in work and deployment international the largest number of people in constellation and is sucessfull and

has served sucessfully and serves today and helps a largest number of people this is the size of the work

which makes a difference and each produce attributes to makes the world a better place. in 2019 the world is

run by computers and used to be run at cabinet

you are a new generation the 3rd generation 1.1.2017. the most important documents are 2 documents, the LEAD the most important document, and The Documents signature the foriegn affairs minister RUSSIA,

the most important document. the bosses of the new generation which is you, yourself male or female or

genuine 1969 or born or rule or solitude or married to god one of 8 000 000 000 people, citicens made for by the geneva convention the new generation 3

lead the way for you and the giant computers do the consumate work and in every case the world includes you

from the time you are 6 months old and we confer infant baptism, conference whence then your society

includes you and excursions are made for handicapped people. The world has achieved a revelation and sucess.

We hope you are comfortable aboard.

our thanks yous are laid at TAIWAN

2026

the world is gunning down the most horrible
people in the world

On the day of attention the worlds greatest
day and the worlds biggest achiement there
was a commoner. the world wont deal with
commoners, i did the dealings, later
for you i installed my people. at the

governor of nsw there was no commoner,
i worked throough it with the governor
and it is true and in 2015 at the
governor nsw record we sealed, i and the
governor also completed bert your defense.
the people in progress were not a commoner
and also philip and vince were recording.
vince is high up, the whole progress
was properly arranged.
the citicens of england set one standard
for themselves and a separate standard for
the citicens in other countries which was
and dire. the record of what was done is
the first actions. following the day of
attention there is a commoner. in councells
by the nations of the world the bosses,
nations gave us an identity. from the
time we will take no measure with a
commoner, i commune with my people is
what i have done, my people have immunity.
excile was built for the rule of the race
of peoples, the rule are theyre bosses.
the nations and union of nations had
0 evidence of repentance assylum was built
for syrria. there are increased results.
because a commoner a lead in the race of
people in the future the balance of the
citicens have immunion against christians
conclusive by the 2016. i retired. i am a
retired scientist . the world wont deal
with commoners. the plans are wicked plans
and the conducts are wicked.
the world doesnt have
the capacity or means to deal with
commoners and whence the commoner is
in place willfully the dealings become
an exclusion. number of the race of
people are condemned. in every case
the race of people are affected by citicens
within the race of people. the race of people
have 0 enemy, the enemy of the race of peope
in the own citicens in the race. the race

face the worlds actions. cost will be in the
race and because of the abhorant conduct of
yhe race there is cost to the race friends
so far over 17 500 important lives, citicens
of USA new mexico peuta rica costa rica the
most of the number died is suply which is
supply ship full nuclear weapons and 12
12 ships supply were blown up, going in
the wrong direction, see archive, i saw
the origin on ABC NEWS 24. kity hawk
            made berth for you and kitty hawk has
5 000 staff and crew aboard, a big cost
if a ship is blown up, kitty hawk dock
in sydney harbour, you can see it all
on cowper wharf road, at harbour bridge,
tourists will have to pay 38AUD for
a packet of cigarettes and a kings ransom
for cigars, the mansion is on
victoria st sydney number one and premium
resturant strip. where it happened is a
building at darlinghust, i showed lucis
the race ive the building, the event
happened at kogorah and changed the world.
the change is for the negative, all the
events i have shown you have changed our
world for the positive have changed our
world for the better and is called
inspiration . in plans QEII and queen mary2
cruise ships passed each other on sydney
harbour and blew the horns one million
people turned up in person to watch as big
as the new years eve fireworks, i watched
from cowper wharf road. you can see
your whole world on the origin and the
search can be done on archive, our whole
world is on dvd thanks to the most
gracious people in the world unbeatable
sucess.

CASH

1966	fund
1976	350
1982	22 500
1986	35 000
1986	International Trading plan

2000	400 000
	75 000 pay out
	750 000
	cinamen 200 000
	cinamen 10 000 000
	rory 15 000 000
	ENOUGH

2000	fbt=0

2002	SALE 280 000 AUD

2010	1 000 000

2010	fbt=700 000

2012	1 000 000

2018	39 accounts 22 000 000
	755 000 PA

2020	1 101 000
	10 800

2020	fbt=680 000

2020	SALE business account 205 000
	PROFFIT 8 470

2022	1 153 000	DRAW 643 000
		OVER 438 000
		147%
		22 000 000 England, York

10 800 balance=0
balance=0
credit=14000
            500
INSURANCE=0
Donation9% paid, in top 10% tax payers since 1990
DEATHS=0
ACCIDENTS-0
42 YEARS
PROFFIT 41%

2022   CREDITORS NOT MET DICTATE
              DISTRIBUTION NOT PAID
              2 STAFF RECORDS OFFICE
              2 ARMY ANOMOLY
              EACH OTHER COMMITMENT HAS BEEN MET

2020   SUPPLY   Minder
              Limousine
              Black Range Rover Retired.HMRH.HMH.BOOKS PHMM. MUSEUM
              8 470 paid to Lalaine

              Ben, what is happened to the race is the race is fallen into a ditch. lets look
              in the holy bible ben, jesus says if the blind lead
              the blind both will fall nto a ditch. aggressor has the biggest risks in the
              world.
              lalaine has lived the life and at the end of the road 2020
              has 26 000 000 in cash and 22 000 000 in account and 1 153 000 in
              137750 and 0 in 5600 and 14 500 credit. lalaine is born and in all lalaine
              has been in charge of there is 0 aggression and
              are results. lalaine had a bad experience with some people and
              an argument with family and for a minute stopped support the family and
              then settled . then lalaine had a bad experience when lalaine
              got a bad infection and was in hospital to be treated with antibiotics and it
              began when lalaine was not allowed to have a cigarette. the doctors made
              many arrangements for lalaine to be at home and finally with a penecillon
              bottle in a pouch the IV lalaine was finally home
              and this was much better. niether one of us would be here without
              st george hospital who treated lalaine for infection and philip for hernia.
              years ago i got the killer flu like the corona virus and wouldnt be here
              without dr tait and his wife of penrith. philip and lucis supported and

cared for lalaine and we steam cleaned the home office, lalaine and lucis
supported and cared for philip we are good carer. we just had a
wonderfull weekend holiday in the city it was perfect and we had plans
and something went in philips back and couldnt move and ruined our
plans
and all the effort was to get me to the physiotherapist and two hours
later i walked out of the physiotherapist, i had to lie down lalaine went into
the city where we were going to stay. lalaine and lucis supported me while
my busted spine wrecked the plans. on the day the world schedule was 0
the world worked for many years toward the worlds biggest day the end of
the work and the production of a whole new planet.
i am walking good again and my bag is packed and im ready to go.but
instead lalaine is coming back from the city because lalaine has a denist
appointment. we missed our timeslot. the offender obstructed the worlds
plans and some of the function and affluence is gone and to get back
the worlds plans is the work the world is doing and as the work is done
is the response . problem is compounded by corona virus moreso
we depend on the work done in the world and the material. in each
generation there has been gracious people in every place in the world
whom have done competent work, i have been one of thier small number
of leading bosses thier works has made the world a vastly better place.
thats how it is ben. god bless.

POST

2000 MILLENIUM

jesus didnt come back, but what the world is doing
is sucessfull the world is doing returns and the
obstacles of the past is overcome and predators
are contained also there is a 50% carbon emmisions
reduction and environmental enhancements.
the world is doing what jesus instructed.
jesus has many name and in each language jesus is described.

1ST JUNE 2019   WORLDS BIGGEST DAY

WE WERE IN WORLDS BIGGEST DAY

1ST JUNE 2020   WORLDS BIGGEST DAY

The world in each generation has for many years
worked towards the worlds biggest day. the world
today is 8 000 000 000 people and there is a hight
of sucess, the work is sucessfull.
generations have worked to make the world a better place
for each citicen and there are improvements and sucess.
the world is always nervous to be sure you are not left
out and further builds to address an individual case.
if you country is good you have sucess, some have
been cheated by a murderer. all the figures are in
monument or memorial in the philippines. 400 years ago
there were 11 murderers. it is long ago and many
years ago the muslims are a murderer the muslim
rules and muslim countries are a great attribute and
contributor in our world and we depend on thier grace.
the islam are the people of the order ie the highest up.
the are 3 murderers in the world and after 28 years
the rebel europeans worst enemy is dead. leaving
2 murders the world nations are in address largely
contained. before the start of the problem the
races were attrite and the numder of the aggressor
from 2009 contained by passage sent by myself the boss
and for 14 years there were no murder/atrocity
0 deaths. the last history is 1990s our achievement
since destroyed by the start. in jesus days there
were also raids the civilisations had to defend from.
the last raid in the world was more than 550 year ago.
jesus spent half of his time dealing with murderers.
saul was the boss of a murderer. the muslim spead
the message then the muslim and the roman catholic
spread the message the bhudist made. the wars in

india were settled.
one commercial-writer was shot. i am a sucessfull
commercial-writer and an bachelor of arms warrant
and writt and a doctor by stamp and a doctor by
line and a boss and a boss of the world and
at the time a leading boss of the world, like the
precious man whom was shot. i do work for the world.
we the people 1% whom run the world have spent half
of all our time dealing with a muderer and for me
the 2 telephones rang 110 times a day for almost
2 years and i worked harder than i have ever worked
in my life before even though some workloads in the past
are so big . i always made it to a destination and
was known as the holiday king, i was always called
lucky phil because my partner was beautifull and as
well intelligent and my life is soaked with lifestyle.
jesus was god and man, i am not jesus, i am a man of
the world a boss and was born, most affluent jesus was
the perfect man, i am a man of the world and so
are the people and woman whom run the world. i was
taught all my time in church a man of the world is about
sex, but this is nothing to do with me, since the monies
were stolen i am all about money and sex, and the other
people whom run the world are all credential. my
partner too was born. we also made it to our destination.
its not over until it is done, it will take 18 years
for the balance of nations to catch up with the
aggressor, beyond my lifetime. this has happened before
in 1980 1990 1999 2002 2006 2013. the start 2009.
stolen monies 2010 2000 and exhtorted monies of
over 330 trillion dollars the account required at
hotel room 7 star saudi arabia where the official was
arrested to to account and has fax machine and we laid
in room defense for the race of people. the official
was arrested from around the world and brought to the
7 star luxury hotel room in 2017 until account is
complete, see news report and archive, this is
the worlds intervention in the 4th generation.
as a boss and as a citicen i shun aggressor.
her majesty instruction 0 aggression is the way for
the race to get through. STAY UNDER BORDER.
i built from the boundaries won at the settlement of

the ww2 and as soon as the race became guilty the
building collapsed and is the most sucessfull
building in the world and the highest outcome in
the world. our planet rely on the balance of
produces and function because of offense in
the kingdom is damaged and offense has destroyed
our capacity everything elso most fortunately
is intact, i am working on function in my assetts,
some of the equipment is not working, the world
depends also on our equipment, some is sophisticated.
equipment. today we are the worlds biggest builder
and we have an arterial plan the sucess remains
but it has been the time of our lifetime working
with the race of people whom we love dearly. we
have close work with each nation and union.
i have lived an active life more than most people do
i have done. i have worn out my joints, my rest of my
body is no1 my body is intact and arteries are clean
and i have full blood flow and function is full,
all good. the joints spine and connection is bad.
my body has made the distance and the science is
reliable, i have had a balanced meal, each meal
and when away had bacon an eggs for breakfast, if
you have the grilled tomato with the bacon and eggs
the tomato breaks down the fat, i was never
overwieght by any amount at all until 41.
i work out doing push ups and sit ups and to
keep my stomach strong eat cabbage. i reguarly ate
prawns lamb and cutlets crustaceans cheescake for
morning and afternoon tea. chinese western menu.
a balanced meal means half meat and half vegetables
and my favourite meal is the roast, the roast is
also the national dish. good for lunch is aussie
hamburger which is beef, lettuce, onion, tomato, beetroot
and you can add extras which is balanced meal.
i also love sandwiches you can build a balance
and sandwich fillings are some of the highest
quality meats, deli meats, i am also a fan
of cheese and love diary products a pure
source and source of calcium, i share chocolate
and arnotts chocolate buscuits,
dark chocolate is health food

and full of antioxidants, and avoid products i
know to have carcenogenics in the products and ate at
a resturant half the time and a resturant in asia.
as children we ate in a resturant half the time.
i always do for meetings and to meet with friends.
a cafe or pub is perfect for lunch steak n vegetables.
any less will short change you body so sometime
2 meals so full are enough in the days and at
time when work commitments are full one big meal
a day. doctors used to eat one meal a day to be free
to meet the demand, now the advice is to make the
big meal at lunchtime so the body burns the fat
but for my partner and many asians more fat is needed.
dad paid for annette 3 times a good father as will of god.
terry paid for nyssa wedding and paid 40 000 the same.
you wont get me im part of the union. we 3 and
I have earned more money than most people can earn.
i have paid for a large amount of work and do a
large amount of work with my partners. as a dignity
i have done each signature and there are diplomatic
embassies. i and cinamen built an empire which today
run sucessfully. i have been in charge of many people
in the worlds work and we have best results and i have
been in charge for the kingdom of england and we have
good results. philip and lalaine retired in 2020.
philip has 16 retirements from work from work in the
world i started and completed 4 service, i have had
2 lifetime given and 2 careers. we are the
longest serving. philip and hays are the youngest
boss in the world and the youngest in the business
and each promotion i am the youngest to be promoted
a unique pathway. i also completed 4 service for
the british empire, productivity supervisor,
built the productivity rows, run
the 17 countries of 53 country commonwealth.
salesman, nuclear retailer sold uranium
and plutionium products to 70 countrys and made
fortunes for the kingdom england york scotland.
ward elizabeth II seat of india, run 6 countries
of england, canada australia south africa for 22 years.
built transmission works. i retired of service
in running the world in 2016. we have 6 homes

and office and an office in hong kong and
usually meet at a resturant and have birthday
and a party at a resturant and love a drive in the car
we also cherrish a view i swam for 40 years and
sometimes 20 laps of the pool and bodysurf the breakers.
i have done figures all my life and have passaged
billions of people and worked hard to be a good boss
how i got to be a good boss, a good life. i have
been boss 75% of my adult work. i worked as a
tradesman 5% of my adult worked and most of the
time i am installed a salesman, our income has
come from business sales and half of our money
to live on comes from investments. we will
with the additional work weapons work 2015 be
paid 4,000,000,000,000 in the era. After 2 days'
the computers will distrinute and the 3 owners will
the same day distribute to the new owners and the
organisations staff have earned 4 000 000 000 000.
50% of the money will be paid out directly a gross
income of 2 000 000 000 000 enough to run the
organisations and pay passage and staff wages/salary
and pay equal to our structure in the world computers.
the cost of event to us is over 220 000 000 000
and from our living 240 000 and for friends
460 000 and my new owners might request
my funders. our banking is 360 000 000 000.
and our household income $1,250,000PA and
after november 2013, in 2014-2022 $242 000 PA
the fanmily i was born in to have 23 farms and
the banking is 26 000 000 000, the birth family face
draught in 2019, each other family have a
livelyhood. we will need to bank more than 3.5%
and for you this is the way to get through, make
sufficient banking. my banking has been enough.
all our commitments are met and only our living
and run the office depend on the monies stolen
by the aggressor, a very good outcome.
it has been a pleasure to work with you.

I BEGAN 1980

NEXT STOP   NEW SENIOR ASSASINS
ARE INSTALED 2025

NEXT STOP   MY ORGANISATIONS
120 YEARS

NEXT STOP   DESTINY 200

All our work is destiny 200 compliance
My Workplace throughout the world is a
handicapped workplace 2004 Compliance.

LAST STOP   4000 AD
Jesus comes back

The world will be run from the lap of god
instead of from a lap-top.
I have worked hard to be a good boss, i am
very organised in keeping the information
and building instruction, a good boss.
the books are opened

---

when it comes to your eternal salvation

the emanuel of the universal god will do
all the work giving your salvation after
you die. never give your life away early.
thank you for reading my book we have
made it to the end.
we were helped as a kingdom by nelson mandella
the world was helped by rose rule taiwan,
amada marcos and dawn chambers my mentor
and philip the monarch, england.,
and the heaven indonesia, brains is in
charge. indonesia is the supply for the
asia pacific region and indonesia built satelites
for india launched. the equipment in the
solar system has a life of 200 years or more.
concrete has a life of 140 years. porsche
metals makes the metals for space, stretch
metal long lasting. be sure you last.

EPILOUGE

THANK YOU FOR BUYING MY BOOK <
THANK YOU FOR THE OPPORTUNITY
TO GIVE YOU THE IMPORTANT
INFORMATION IN A NICE WAY.
I KNOW FROM EXPERIENCE YOU
WILL BE BETTER EQUIPED TO FIND YOUR WAY AROUND
IN OUR PRECIOUS WORLD. Philip.

Sufficient WORK
2020
Workplace DIGNITY
Workplace HERE
MY STAFF Are the only Persons in the World
WHOM DO PART OF THE WORK Of The PEOPLE Born TO IT>
ONE PART OF PARTS AND COMPONENTS.
Designed and built over 2 centuries after 2 centuries
each time the people whom did it were not sucessfull,
i undertook the work and we did it and we were
sucessfull, the first time the people were sucessfull
and the work was done, the work was much needed in
the world and much was failing so much attention was put
in to getting the work done and the work up but didnt
sucessfull, we achieved to do the work and was sucessfull
and was a great celebation and there is vastly more
function in the berths in the world, over the years
these has resulted in function in communities as well
as other benefits a the world also turned back the
launch on iran indonesia which would have dire
consequences and outcomes and for the first time in
years we would be heading for the end, when i grew
up the world was going to blow up, and we learnt to plead.

ireland U2 bon scott and the boys are sucessfull, there
is also a minor mitigation by australias midnight oil
and is part of the worlds testament and a component of
the education in the world to every generation peter garret
also served as senator. i from 1991-2014 was the boss
but the work done by my organisations is a work place.
we kept carefull records and achieved to do the workload
a second time and also we earned money and had enough money
to make it on our own, we had 240 000 staff, by then it was 1988.
in 1990 we made a second plan. the work done contributed to
dramatically increased worlds results like jesus wanted
the level of - love each other and by 2000 you made it.
my staff were awarded and the confidence was made the
work was IMPORTANT. i have been working on growing the
number of staff the working on growing the number of
staff all the time . my staff have a big surprise- all
the time i have been working on grownig staff, the staff
have been building offices. we got more results. my staff
have long qualifications and have good education and are expert,
by the time i have finished my studies i am expert. i also
own ELECTRIC LABORIORY. It is one of the worlds sucess stories
and appreciate being owners. we are now founder of a number
of organisations. i am known as a good organiser and i have
also been a good organiser for the kingdom of england, britain
and the british empire, 141 countries. i have bee boss of the
world a long time and served people now 8 000 000 000 people
and in our time there is a service for animals, you have a
nice world. in my work we are 1,100,000 people and is a
workplace and my work place is called HERE and the office
is in the kingdom of england. Each part of the workplace
have a name given and made by the staff and a name given by me.
we also have nicknames. there has been severial events in my
workplace .on the day of event no names were made
and no devotion was done and after the world found what was
done and what happened i have had help with staff security
by the people who lead and do the world and security agencies.
i built the staff security myself since 1982 and the security has
been sucessfull, my/our staff have had 0 deaths and 0 accidents
from 1982 to 20.11.2013 the security i built myself and i have a
profound reputation. i also did the insurance for our work in each
country and i have a C.V. . I stuck with the same insurer since 1982.
I have had the same employer, employers 26 years, very fortunate we

all are. philip and lalaine have a good workplace which is a cool business.
we should thank you for your help with staff security. to address the
monies stolen the nations of the world put on nearly 1500 INVESTIGATORS
one for each country we operation in and the investigators build SUPPLY
to the bosses. to be a boss you must be born because the born do the
work of run the world, planet, universe, nations. we the world
now 8 000 000 000 people citicens got to where we are because of
GRACIOUS people, and was 2 500 000 people. the people in thailand
are lovely the people in the philippines are nice we have been to
the most exciting places in the world. luke built the most sustain known
in the world . luke was a doctor whom live in the place at the time. luke
was loyal and built a carefull record like a doctor living in england
empire london descendent city in the day was ruled by assyria empire.
luke loyal made a whole new world possible and is today the gospel
according to luke. our book is work and part of the worlds testables
the holy bible is the worlds testable and the worlds chronicles and
luke the doctor record. it can be done where the loyal kept carefull
records and on the day of attention the 8 000 000 000 world achieved
the biggest achievements in the 16 500 000 000 years history of the
world. we got there by keeping loyal information store and record.
RED HERRING VS HERRING, GERMANY AUSTRIA IS THE EPICENTRE BORDERS
ARE BEING BUILT IN THE AFRICAN CONTINENT THE REBEL ARE DEAD AND
100% of ALLY
ARE HOME, ENTER CORONA VIRUS THE TOLL 360 000 People 0.00045-0.0009% of
The worlds population, The largest number dead are acts of god,
thence the aggressor murders, thence the rebel, thence corona virus,
thence shortfall in community services, from you understanding of the
incorruptable god and what goes up must come down and love for each other
a huge number of lives, important function, livestock and animals have
been saved by flooding and the world saved 2 billion lives plus rescues.in
event saved half the lives and measured the global financial crisis
and people live longer have more housing, a vegetable garden in space
and have more babies and achieved 0 war between countries, the plan.
the world is a better place and the world is on its way to saving
3 billion lives and is building to feed 20 billion people. pure dreams,
concious work and a life of grace, congratulatios.

i needed my statistics man and 2 office records staff
the region and kingdoms needed the appartment bayswater
the world needed the belt belt2, dictate
england needed the defense work done, the monies settled
and dictate to do the distribution, distribution done 4.5m,
creditors paid, claims paid, claims dawn paid, victims
compensations paid, depiction writing done, response,
in the 6 years response, act. act minister for services,
not a snowflakes chance in hell.
456 000 paid councelled 2 times, 156 000 paid councelled
2 times.
not possible.8 years work. our cost 81 000 PA. fees $10.
each has been dealt with. the best results in
the history of the kingdom of england, a quality defense.
there is o written thank you. there is a return warrant.
the human courts handed down against 600 000 000 and on
the return warrant the race is disposed. the problem
was conduct. THE RECORDS ARE THE HUMAN COURT RECORDS.
the account was done by charles massih + co.
name + citicen ship is laid at world table by nations.
the highest number of dead in the history of modern
arms and so our memory. in memory of proffessor chueng
and our loved ones and mama. the attribute dean chambers
survey of arms.1991. i thank my dictate and eave.
the race needed the 2 army personel present. i n
memory of the condilisa daughter.1999 and the
ambassador wife philippines and the united nations
officials the whole world and animals depend on 2013.
a signal of the rosemary, the attestant steve and rose.
my office is in hong kong. we never go into the office
see the british series absolutely fabulous for a
depiction see the life of brian for fun see the
american series married with children, for the
journey of a life see michael palin, for interest
see dan cruickshank around the world in 80 treasures,
for us see harry borman by any means, for the berth and
secret year see my chemical romance dvd available at
jb hi fi east gardens,
the world cadillac and memory. the education was
supplied by the blues brothers. the chinese democracy

tour is the gerth and the providence is guns and roses
use your illusion 1 and use your illusion 2, you ll nevr
get luck out of life if you stay a mortician forever man.
the episode was greenday on stage, greenday in sydney
and greenday in japan, and the dictation is indiana jones
theme and the crusade livin' thing ELO, the meeting is
elton john 40 years celebration of rocket man and the
testables were signed by norma jean riley stage name marylin monroe.
years of work. australia 60 years figures are done among many
other works and are on dvd 2 men in china at all good music stores,
i am the producer, i built the passage and did the passaging.
norma jean signed for the universe before the first verses of
peace existed, the distribution was done by the citicens
generation of taiwan, the western world. the work was done
on video by christine applegate and friends. the instruction
is at tahiti an aerial on tower and warragamba port 2000. the
translation and design is red october 1982.the instruction
is the writing of the commercial-writers, the new world.
QUIVER
in past of this world the quiver was all the weapons available
and held to a verse or a throne, look at the huge difference in
in the quiver the world has built from and worked from. god bless.
a changed world for the better and posotive, congratulations.
the fig is hubble telescope. god the universal god built the
existing fig, the north pole and the south pole. we wish you peace.

THE BOOK SHOWS THE WORLD IS GHANGED FOR THE BETTER
AND THERE IS MORE BENEFITS, IT TOOK EVERYONE IN THE
WORLD TO DO IT. AND THERE IS MORE ; IT HAS GONE GOOD,
IT TOOK EVERYONE IN HEAVEN AND ON EARTH TO DO IT OR
WE WOULD NOT BE HERE. SUCH ARE THE OUTER BOUNDARIES
AND INSIDE THERE IS A SECRET. SUCH IS THE REPORT AS
COMPLICATED AS YOU A STRAIGHT SHOOTER AND WINNER.
YOU HAVE A CORRECT WEAPON DIRECTION AGAINST THE
ASTRAY, MORE BENDS THAN A BANANA. POOR JOB.
JOB WAS A RULER WHOSE CIVILISATION LOST ALL
AND IT WASNT HIS FAULT OR THIER FAULT AND
WAS NOT A VENGENCE. POOR JOB IS SUFFER FROM
AND AGGRESSOR AND MANY TIME THE INNOCENT
SUFFER FROM DROUGHT OR STORM. PERU HAD
30 YEARS OF DRAUGHT THEN 30 YEARS OF FLOODING
AND COULDNT MAKE IT. NOW THE WEATHER SYSTEM HAS

SLOWED DOWN CALL ELNINO AND ELNINIO. THE WEAPONS
DIRECTION YOU HAVE DONE WILL GIVE YOU THE BETTER
CHANCE AND JOB, THE COUNTRIES WHOM SUFFER.

dear ben, thank you for giving me the lattitude to
use up your time and twist your ear off, over time
you will be confident in mr malcolm vision.

We have got everything.
We put in a premium order and pay postage and select
insurance cover to deliver to destination 50 shades
of gray and hope you have enjoyed living
the high road to china.

REPORT PLANET AUTOBIOGRAPHY

Celebrating 40 years

FROM 16 I DO FIGURES FOR A LIVING
for 20 YEARS I SUPPLY HOME and in the
money I supply Home a long Time to
august 2020 Janet birthday. Janet
started the FUND in 1966.
The RULE Aligned Together In 1956
the Signature was done at The Table At
Strathfield. We have the Fortune and the Photograph.
Sometimes in this world the Documents are a Photograph.
The Kidd Family was in it because John Married My Mother.
It is Time to Move to OLD BAR. Lalaine was First in Sydney 2009
and has Good Years and We are PAID TO 2024.
Lalaines Family is Good and at End of Records
september 2020 Survived Corona Virus.
WE HAVE A DIGITAL STORE
WHITE PHILIP KIDD - SPACE
The Solution on Our Website is

INCOME RECIEPTED

4 020 000 000 000

MONIES STOLEN > 10.2 B

PROFFIT 8470

3 972 000 000 000 2012-2018

AFRICA BORDERS 80 000 000 PA

HOBBY PURPOSE 120 B PA

NETT 1 596 856 725

AUS BUSINESS COMPONENT

ROI 511M + 23 550 000

HOUSEHOLD INCOME

242 000 PA

england account 22 000 000

we have jurisdiction in 240 39 191 countries we respond to written searches the search fee made in cheque in AUD from

the Institue Office Lively records. There is a REPORT in each Nation in each Year. All our works is done in the WORLD COMPUTER in Which we have built since 1976

since 1982. Found in 1980 of importance is our assets which benefit each person in the world now 8 000 000 000.

and service animals. In our time Global Warming Content is reduced by 50% and we contribute to the Maintainance of Global Warming Reductions.

We are also one of the worlds leading nuclear experts. We work for each Nation and Union of Nations how we achieve to make a benefit for all people in the world and our primary offices span the planet and we can get work done. We are continually building. Philip is a Successful Commercial-writer and has run the 6 biggest developments for the world. The

people whom do the work of developments are in alignment called celestial. We aligned with

Elizabeth Hilton the people whom in alignment are the developer called celeste and together we are the worlds biggest builder. Philip kidd space and the people are an individual entity.

Our other corums are staff devoted to citicens experience.

The world has 6 improvement in the 2nd generation and a better world and have achieved the same countries borders. less have died and people live longer. Lalaine and Philip are region and region. Philip is Rocketman and was the former region technical rocketmen. Berlin and Philip own the 10 Barristers which each service person has travelled in in majatron the 1st side of the world or rocketman the 2nd side of the world. Lalaine has the most success

entity born in 15 generations 100% of the Ally 3 is made it home. The world has seen the greatest achievments in the history of the world and people have more babies. The world population explosion is a result of success and is to be embraced not feared.

The worlds first work is security just like for thousands of years. The worlds 2nd work because of success is to feed 20 billion people work is already underway we always have plenty to do. The work of the world is run and done in writing and serves each person one day to be 20 000 000 000

people the global family. The articulation is done inside a computer. By 2019 after

35 years of building the world is run by giant computers. Philip worked to supply home from

1980-2000 and we had a successful home we earnt 28 000 000 and our organisations were paid 940 000 000 AUD which we invested in our organisations. We have met the worlds demand and I have grown double the number of staff in each world calendar.

If you work from the report your nation has not obscured secret the same as we do and as we do the work for each nation and race. we work for 27 000 races. lalaine and Philip

earned 2 800 000 from engagements. We made it in 2020 we have done allright lalaine is a beautifull partner. I am a good husband as lalaine expresses our time. We had an affluent life. we have had a large amount of monies stolen each and every transit, we now live a luxury life and lalaine supports our family for a retirement whom is middle class. We have 5

properties to live in and for office and a weekender. 3

are beachouses and we have had a life by the sea and good friends. lalaine has paid and paid for 4 years. our organisations are paid to 2024.

we are paid to 2022. lucis is paid. the rule is paid. the citicens are paid for the nation wall. Writing is complete at governor of NSW 2015. Our organisations have 494 properties in total and STORE

DOWNLOAD MY FULL RESUME C.V.
RESUME
PUBLICATIONS Life Story 2
New Page

WITHOUT LIVING AND WORKING IN THE BLUE MOUNTAINS I WOULD NEVER HAVE LEARNT EMERGENCY. I ENDED UP RUNNING EMERGENCY. ONE OF THE WORLDS BIGGEST EMERGENCY THE BOY - KING RAN AND MY STUDY ALIGNMENTS ARE NAMED AFTER THE NAME OF THE Boy-King, INTUIT. OUR HISTORY IS TUIT.
I HAVE RUN EACH EMERGENCY WHICH HAS COME UP THE LADDER TO ME, SUCESSFULLY.

I started off in 1976. I was 16. We were BUILDING. IN 1982 I Was Given 60 000 000 000 all taxations settled by a Ruler for a PURPOSE. I BUILT THE OFFICE AT HONG KONG. 1980
I Was
Installed REGION TECHNICAL. In 2000 I was MADE Region. CINAMEN AND I BUILT AN EMPIRE. LALAINE AND I HAVE BEEN RUNNING THE OFFICES SUCESSFULLY. I HAVE DONE A GOOD JOB IN
THE GLOBAL
STATE OF NATION. I HAVE DONE A GOOD JOB. NOW 44 YEARS. I HAVE PAID 42 YEARS. I AM A SUCEESFULL
Commercial - Writer. I Am now Retired. Lalaine is Rteired After The Work is Finished and After Working a sixth job because
monie is stolen which would be our outcome in personal account. CUT OFF BY WORK DONE BY NATIONS I HAVE WEAPONS WORK 2015.

BEAUTIFULL STORY VS BAD A STORY OF 8 000 000 000 PEOPLE.

WE ARE AWARDED AND I HAVE THE HIGHEST AWARDS. I WAS GIVEN THE INFORMATION ON WHAT WENT ON BY THE NATIONS IS HOW WE HAVE KNOWN HOW TO RUN THE ALIGNMENTS.

THE NATIONS FOUND OUT WHAT WAS DONE AND IS HISTORY NOW. I AM PAID.

PORT MAQUARIE BEACHOUSE IS OUR PRIMARY RESIDENCE. IN 1976 LIVE CORPORATE ENGAGED OUR FIRST CLIENTS. ALL ACCOUNTS ARE INTACT.

WE HAVE PLENTY OF MONEY ENOUGH MONEY BUT LITTLE LEFT FOR OUR LIVING MONEY BECAUSE PHILIP AND LALAINE HAS HAD A LARGE AMOUNT OF MONEY STOLEN

THOSE LAID BY NAME + CITICENSHIP BY THE Nations AT THE WORLD TABLE HAVE NOT BEEN RELEVENT. WE WENT A LONG WAY TO PRODUCING FOR THE RACE and IN THE SEAT Of INDIA

HAD THE 4-6 MOST RESULTS IN THE WORLD For the 6 Countries, Destoyed by citicens of england 2004-2020, You Can Be PROUD OF THE BALANCE OF CITICENS. IT IS TIME FOR

AN OLD SHEEP ADDAGE. BECAUSE THE BOSS OF THE RACE IS CALLED SHEPPARD THE Citicens is Called SHHEP. THE EAST PRECINCT WON.

ALSO IN THE END THE WORLD WON AGAINST CITICENS WHICH ALIGNED THEMSELVES AS AN AGGRESSOR. RUSSIA DO MY 21 SOLICITORS FOR ME.

PHILIP + HAYS SUPPLY THE NATIONS ORDER and HANDS RUSSIA. Philip Has a SPACE LICENCE, Philip Maintained his licences.

Philip paid the big money, Cigarettes rose from 120 pw paid to 260 pw a carton of

200. this compares with a family shopping bill

of 240 pw or 3000 pa to run a car original. Tolls rose. We paid for 3 people. It is a big challenge to hold every LITTLE persons HAND in the world So Big.

There is now enough information and enough in formation to run a country. all country. Union of Nations is the Nations People Whom Live on Islands.

We also help maintain the archipelego Cisis, the worlds Newest Continent. philip is a Governor of Crisis and the Citicens Elected MAYOR. Crisis

is the Former USSR TERAIN. The world has a Miracle Result, A BIG ACHIEVEMENT. After the this big battle we have GOT EVERYTHING and We Have MADE IT and

The WORK Continues, there is some new assets 4M.

\We are MISSING,

HOUSE

RECORDS OFFICE

REGION LAY-OUT

RETIREMENT MONIES

BELT, BELT 2 missing from NATIONS CITICENS

LOVED ONES

TIME, FREEDOM DICTATED

more of them so the nations actions for more of them

WE HAVE MADE UP THE REST AND ALSO WE HAVE NEW VAULTS

THE BEST PEOPLE

Ive retired now the telephone no longer rings since 2016/2017 and the NATIONS SETTLED, AND SETTLED With New generation 2018 and as OWNER I sealed all taxations.

There were 0 telephone calls and the triens wre up and running and there were o blow-ups

and the triens were running by 2019. there was after 2018 no more renumeration and all my projects are close

and lalaine and philip have finished engagements and in 2020 have a total of income we got in and known costs.

the work is finished and we retired hosting 2020 has to be done. It is a shock when you see the end it is so good

better. All the work is Done and is Improvement in BENEFITS AND FORTIFIES BENEFITS for EACH CITICEN.

ALSO WE CAN PROVE BECAUSE OF THE MOST AFFLUENT RESULTS THE PLANS OF THE GENERATIONS BEFORE ARE GOOD PLANS.

We were fortunate to get the work done before the destruction is impelling. THE RESULTS ARE BEST.

I CAN TELL YOU WHERE THE RESULTS CAME FROM, WE ARE SO FORTUNATE TO BE IN CHARGE OF GOOD PEOPLE - THE BEST PEOPLE.

The Relation cannot be solved to CURE because of IMPACT the corona virus, the last LEG for BENEFITS for CITICENS.

As Instructions workload pertains to the Event and we can get little work done the opposite to before.

There is little work hours for projects which as in the most on hold and the Hours are Devoted to the GLOBAL STATE Of NATION.

Such is the big changes in our world the DIRECTION of THE NATIONS. When done the

DIRECTION which is the lead in the world is ABOUT WEAPONS,

I EXPLAIN THE WEAPONS WORK 2015. I WAS APOINTED AND INSTALLED TO DO THE WEAPONS WORK, WHICH IS THE WEAPONS WORK FOR EACH NATION.

MY STAFF WILL DO THE WORK, I HAVE BUILT SUPPLY SO I CAN SUPPORT. WE WILL DO THE WORK FOR EACH NATION AND NONE WILL BE LEFT OUT.

I HAVE A Business Photographs ALBUM. All the Information Contribute to Report. IT IS A PLEASURE TO BE IN CHARGE IN THE YEARS OF ACHIEVEMENT.

REPORT 1

REPORT 1 2020

REPORT 2000

REPORT 1980

LAUNCH 1976

FUND   1966

1986 EAST PRECINCT

1991 APPOINTED IN SEAT Of INDIA

2000   RECIEPTS MILLENIUM

2014 = 0

Lifes Story, FAMILY TREE.

WE HAVE 494 PROPERTIES

6 Properties To Live in and Office.

ALL MY PEOPLE HAVE RETIRED AND ARE A NEW GENERATION.

I HAVE MET 1/3 OF THE NEW GENERATION.

The old Generation called reguarly, the new generation dont call.

its a quiet life. The REGION Together Call.

Our work will be done by searches untill the time all our work worldwide is done IN-PERSON and Also the REGION developement has such EFFECT as the Work is done IN-PERSON

and the REGION Developements is Sucessfully.

WE OWN CAMP ACROSS BORDERS WILL STAY. I HAVE NO MORE PARTNERSHIPS>

PEOPLE

I am retired now. I have 1.3 MILLION PEOPLE AND STAFF. Philip and Lalaine Run the Offices. The ORGANISATIONS ARE FULLY SERVICED.

WE are Region, Region and I am Senior Assasin to 2025 When The WORLD Install New Senior assasin. Where I am A citicen Frank Sator is ASSASIN.

THE BEST PEOPLE. Philip and Berlin Have CHAINS GALILEO, we Founded FINGERTIPS IN SPACE

- RESARCH INTO DARK ENERGY and PHILIP KIDD - SPACE OWNS U.V.GALAXY
also I OWN GALACTIC. I have treasured my partnerships i have had starting at 16 and the partnerships has been sucessfull.

MY WRITING IS IN TERRAIN And Worked From, Fluent. My Staff Built and do PRESENTATIONS to the NATIONS 50% of our nett proffit from 20 x it costs us but are part of the devotion which changed the world. The persons

in work are Competent and Reliable. I also signed in the Floors, BERTHS ONE LOVE. The RACES ADVANCE see the REBEL DEAD After 28 Years following the Terror ATTACK

MUNNION TOWER in 1991. Lucis SIGN the Defense for the RACE England, Lucis OWN Race. I finished the records in RECORDINGS and BOOKS. As a BOSS I WAS COUNCELLED BY IRELAND HALL ALL THE YEARS I DID WORK AS A BOSS.

AS A LEADER ALL MY WORK IS DONE IN SAFES. THE WORK IS ON DVD. THE WORK FOR England is ON VIDEO LIBRARY the Persons are On My LIBRARY.

STORY 1980-2020 IN BLACK LEATHER GLOVES. Presentation Equipment 272 000.

I HAVE DONE EACH WORK AS THE DIGNITY. WE HAVE SIGNED THROUGH A WHOLE PLANET.

[for ye formal christians - WHOM GOD INCARCERATION SEND] I EXPLAIN THE UNIVERSAL GOD-GOD Is Also Peoples and angels,

for people on Earth the Marathon is The SAINTS. In a Signature The GOD is 8 000 000

000. GRAPHICS which our world is Run From Is BUILT BY DEVOTING All 8 000 000 000 ARE WISE-WISDOM and has been done this way for at least 13500 years.

CALLED CERTAIN.

I have signed through with my witness as my ancestors did A WHOLE PLANET as your future will the highest OFFICE in EARTH.

I have signed through with my witness a whole planet the population has grown. I did each Signature, we laid each FILE,

I BEGUN IN SIGNATURE WITH MY WITNESS THE WORK IN THE UNIVERSE, EACH WORLD WORK THE PRESENT AT FORK N' VIEW. I HAVE DONE EACH INSTALLATION. I WITH LALAINE SIGNED THROUGH THE WHOLE UNIVERSE AT MAKATI and Signature BEGUN THE WORLDS WORK RIGHT THROUGHOUT THE UNIVERSE, a Big Undertaking and following the BEST Results LAID By HOST and I have Made a Story with each one Kicking off a world of sucess

. THEYRE BILLIONS OF DOLLARS SPEND WISELY, VERIFIED BY THE OUTCOMES, and Additional ASIA - PACIFIC REGION 2 SAFES, and the NATIONS 2 SAFES, RECORDED. IT IS A VAST THING TO SEE A BETTER WORLD. ALL FROM 1 MODERN HOME OFFICE AND 1 CHAIR The worlds work in our universe in all new generations which starts in our lifetime but serves in generations beyond our lifetime. The Nations have Been BUILDING my CHAIR 2001 since 2001

and for 8 000 000 000 THE PRODUCE, THE BUILDING FLYS IN SPACE- REGISTERED TO OWNERS AND THE CALLATERAL WORLD SURVEYLANCE. DOBLE DOORS. MY 1 ST JOB I HAVE DONE FOR 40 YEARS and MY ORGANISATIONS ARE CELEBRATING 40

YEARS. I HAVE 14 LOVED ONES are 2 PARTNERS, Family in the Philippines. are 4 children and partners from 4 bloodlines, the Parents are cant find work - which means retired in ENGLISH.

IN MY Lifetime I HAVE BEEN IN CHARGE OF SOME OF THE WORK AS THE WORLDS SENIOR ASSASIN AND I HAVE SEEN THE WORK BE SUCESSFULL.

In ENGLISH a new generation of ministers in aboriginal terms and new Lay-Out for The elders to be specific.

I HAVE PASSAGED BILLIONS OF PEOPLE and for years worked as a staff to supply home SUPERVISION. I saved up for a house to turn into a HOME.

MY PARTNER LALAINE 2008 IS INVESTOR. PHILIP HAS FUNDERS.

PHILIP AND HAYS IS WORLD HISTORIAN, HAYS IS NORMAL. Philip and Hays Are the Youngest In The Business.

We have been a participant in the World saving 2 000 000 000 lives, In ENGLISH CALLED SOULS.

In ENGLISH - a Boss of the World, EXTENSIVE OWNER, SERVICE, PRESENT DIGNITY I am Called

RETIRED SCIENTIST.

Senior Assasin is My Job and Owner and Owner 2008. Philip and Lalaine are Region and Region.

Philip is Head, Of Secret service 2nd SIDE of The World.

Read our family Story in the Birth years.

THE WORLD DECIDED TO BUILD REGIONS IN 1980 and The result is a better world on top of the result a better world,

and Reconcilliation Tables, REACH.

OUTCOME

DOCUMENT 1
DOCUMENT 2
DOCUMENT 2-2 foriegn Affairs minister RUSSIA.

I was Educated in england we were educated to do what it takes to make the world a better world in high school,

consistent with my devoted educations. Some of you have had a secret, there is an education in ROCK MUSIC!

Ancestors

My Birth Family in Generations BUILT the Boundaries Thence Chambers For the 2nd SIDE of the World thence Later Bound and Laid HALLS in my

generations Laid ground for the Modern University and was in the Parts, when Australia was Established moved from Europe to australia, and built Homes,

French Nobility and established I was Born to It 2 Times.

When I was 20 years old I went to Drummoyne Sailing Club for dinner. I enjoyed dinner very much. When I had finished dinner I said I enjoyed dinner very much.

the Man started Talking to Me. I Was made an invitation to Dinner the next week to continue the conversation. I changed my plans and went back the next week.

Later these Men helped me by faxing these Men wanted to help me in the work wherein I was Born to It. These Men the 1000's have faxed all over the world for me.

We have together served and lived a lifetime. These Gracefull Men paid for each works. There was problem on the day IN ATTENTION. The Nations of the World are now starting to be in address. the 2nd SIDE of the World is developed and there is A Governance Installed. the problem is no dictate, monies.

I retired at 57, My Retirement Produces, all is substantial and all produces BUT MONEY IS STOLEN. The Inputs in Computers are open. The world is investigating.

We work up $ 1,450,000 in the 10 years. Lalaine has Liberty equal to the retirement. We made it in the Worlds BIG DAY and MADE IT IN GOOD HEALTH. WE ALL HAVE MET OUR OBLIGATIONS AND COMMITMENTS. TO REDEEM MONEY INSTRUCTIONS ARE CEASED.

I STILL RUN A BUSINESS, THE PEOPLE OF A BUSINESS. $410 000 INVESTED 64 YEARS.

MY PEOPLE ARE NOW RETIRED. I RAN THE MISSIONS IN EUROPE, CHARITY IS RUNNING THE RETURN MISSIONS IN EUROPE.

The money is owned by Philip, Cinamen, Lalaine. cinamen has an independent money in the girls effort.

Each person engaged has had money to work from.

PRI IS IN CHARGE

MY PRIORITY IS IN CHARGE

There has been 750 000 people in CAMP. Charity has 250 000 people in CAMP on the North Border. Berlin recovered the borders in Europe. The nations of the World

Gracious work - citicens doing work from the Figures Saved 1/2 the Lives SUPPLY ECONOMY. I never do any of the work myself even tho I have all the Work Recorded and all the Calculations done. MY MAN WHITE,

or MY PEOPLE or MY STAFF DO AND FOR THE Nations, NATHAN My HEAD Of STAFF as Nathan has done in Produce. I also

have competent records. I am to be the boss and not to be engaged, I am a good boss and I am entirely hands on.

I instead have made account for the Nations from the record of the Work done by Nations. I have used up all my hours.

\We have cooked in to save money a complete change for us and I have cooked meals for 3 years and passed blood tests.

OUR CONSTABLES WITH CHINA WE OWN THE ACROSS BORDERS CAMP. WE HAVE HUMMERS IN THE TABLES OUR WORK IS DONE INSIDE

A HUMMER FULL ARMERY BUILT 1999 BY PHILIP AND PEACE.

2 Billion Lives saved

WE TOGETHER HAVE OCEAN GALAXY U.V. SURVEY. THE ULTRA VIOLET SURVEY CAN SEARCH LAND BOUND FOR THOUSANDS OF KILOMETERS

HOW SO MANY LIVES ARE SAVED AND WITH THE ULTRA VIOLET SEARCHES WERE MAPPED A LOGISTIC WAS BUILT AND THE VEHICLES

ARRIVE LAND BOUND AND PICKED UP THE CHILDREN, HOW THE CHILDRENS LIVES WERE SAVED IN LOWER EUROPE. THE CHILDREN WAS OTHERWISE EMBEDDED BY THE REBELS.

U.V. GALAXY SEARCH AND ULTRA VIOLET SURVEY IS USED FOR MANY OTHER WORKS A PART OF THE WORLDS SUCESS IS BUILT AND OWNED

BY OUR ORGANISATIONS A SUPPLY TO THE CITICENS OF THE WORLD.

We Have Many Projects in the Universe.

We Have Projects in the Solar System.

We Are Rulers.

Our Business is Done From

The Protocols

Space Station

I own The Proceedure of The Business

1/2 the Lives Saved

We Run a good SHIP With My Employee DOLLY And My Sectretary SANDRA.

A PRIVATE CHARTER
ALL ABOARD

COMPASSIONS REEF, COOK

Philip Kidd

CAREER OBJECTIVES I am looking for employment at an organisation where I can use my current skills, and learn and develop new skills. I believe my strong people skills, ability to multi-task and liaising on all levels would suit any employer looking for a skilled employee. My positive traits include attention to detail, and my ability to learn quickly and liaise on all levels. People describe me as ambitious, enthusiastic, and energetic. I feel these attributes would help me succeed in a variety of roles.

Sucessfull Commercial - Writer

EMPLOYMENT HISTORY   SALESMAN SALESMAN Energy Retail Sales   Nuclear Products +SUPPLY Awarded Salesperson Experience In

PHILIP J. KIDD

1982-2018 C.V. Boundary, International, SPACE Australia Grid Boundaries, Vietnam Grid SALESMAN 1996-2014 B.E. Retaliation Salesperson 1976-1981 First Career Share Reticulations, PARTY $940,000,000 AUD INVESTED

ELECTRICAL+ INVESTMENT Investment Era II, Investment 4 Staff Education Presentations Owner, Books, Costs defense Coroners Reports 861 Countries Insurance Properties STRATA REPAIR $3,972,000,000HKD 2012-2018 PAID ROI=160,000,000AUD 161,000,000AUD 191,000,000AUD BANKING SAME EMPLOYER, EMPLOYERS 26 YEARS

SELF INSURED

 STAFF AWARDED

OUR ORGANISATION HAS SAVED the MOST LIVES IN THE WORLD, OUR PRECIOUS WORLD for the
3RD TIME IN A ROW
2006 2009 2009 2012 2012 2015
and the Staff and My Seniors have been awarded.
I was on more than 100 trials each 100 deeds from woman, cleared trial. Most unfortunately the installations of england failed trial 2016.

In mach 2013 I was on trial when the staff wages were stolen. more than 1,116 trials have arisen from november december 2013.

there were >1400 claims on me in the appartment on the day of hosting and ticking every box, my insurer paid out.

there are over 7.500.000.000 victims, there was evacuation and the secret service

aligned claims, some claims still persist.

this was the start of the state of nation, there were 0 claims before and there is

0 claims since and my INSURANCE = 0.

The state of Nation grew and is the biggest problem the world has had to address in more than 400 and more than 600 years

but the effect, IMPACT of the corona virus BUG-COVID could be as big a problem the world has to address. The Conduct was abhorhent.

Philip and Lalaine and Lucis Did the WORK. Some of the victims are our Best Friends. Where the Monies is DIASTURBED We are Victims

and Have a Fortified Claim also after the event I get HELP with STAFF SECURITY and

WHEN MY STAFF 140000 England Wages were Stolen

The REGIONS Help with Money and for the Purpose of Getting the WORK DONE The REGIONS ALIGNED MY STAFF UN-PAID ON REGION SALARIES.

The Court cases Stil Ensue. Since the time in 2013 I have spent 1/2 my life in court the biggest Change. THERE IS BIGGER CHANGE

AND THE HOPE WE ALL HAVE A VASTLY BETTER WORLD WHERE MOST PEOPLE LIVE AND PEOPLE LIVE LONGER AND HAVE MORE BABIES THE FOUNDATION

Of OUR FUTURE. This Is The START OF THE BIGGEST CHANGES IN MODERN TIME. TODAY OUR LIFE IS NOT THE SAME BECAUSE WE RESPONDED.

ORDER WAS SETTLED BY MY VALLEY NUNN. MANSIONS BECAME Independent.

We are a household after 2014=0 of household income $ 242 000 PA a rich household, before our household income was

$1,250,000 PA we will go broke in our home and office between 2022 and 2026. Everything else is paid for and we

have everything and have good days. We hope you have it good. We had an Affluent Life, Now without the monies settled we have a Luxury Life.

Most of the Work is Done.

1980-2018

Lalaine Paid as region and Lalaine has Paid in Full, All our friends Paid, All the

Victims paid, The Commerce Board

in The Philippines Signed through in signature the Governance of South america

Continent, The Generations have Banking You can expect it double better. Sucessfull,

I am a Commercial-writer, Sucessfull commercial-Writer all the work was done to make the writing sucessfull.

I worked to put a roof over my head and did SUPPLY HOME it was sucessfull 20 years. The Staff of the Organisations was Built. The staff of the Organisation Supply

Supervision for the Nations

of the World make Produce the WORLDS first INTER-NATION Boundaries and has been enourmously sucessfull

people live MUCH longer for a 3rd time my staff my Staff have saved the most number of lives in the world and

are AWARDED. We have every Award.

IN 2012 WE saw installed and Run Up New Economies of the World.

IN 2012 Everthing was Paid for, I and My Sister Nursed my Father and My Sister attendended all his needs paid

by the compensation board which my father built when my father ran the seat of India. Terry was a Constant.

Terry is Reknown for His love and BBQ's.

IN 2010 The monies were not settled there became PROBLEM. The People of Our Precious Planet PUT 1500

INVESTIGATORS ON and Did Work and Supply to HELP Me. The Investigators WORK PAYS OFF

for the citicens

of the World >7 500 000 000 and philip and lalaine the Victims are very fortunate to have investigators on

working in our monies, I faced a bad offender 19 years since the 1st monies were stolen. I finished the commitment IN 2018 and the RECORDS are BUILT. I could not pay out and

was on a growning number of

trials. The INVESTIGATORS 1500 LAID GROUNDS FOR ME IN EACH TRIAL AND I WAS CLEAR OF TRIAL we have have lived on savings.

The Figures are TAXATION CLAIMS England York Scotland Australia, Samoa, Australia $ 34,445,618 AUD 2018.

I WAS INSTRUCTED BY THE NATIONS TO BUILD ASSETTS REGISTER 2018. The Balance of Figures is 2/3 PLY'S.

WE ALSO DO WORK FOR THE NATIONS. THE COST FROM MY WALLET FOR OFFICE IS 19.5M FBT=680

000 FBT 2000-2010 700 000

AND IS ALSO THE SAME AS THE TRIAL, Assembly England Concord. In the Trials Erroneous

Ground was Laid by

England York scotland Citicens in congestion. The Search of records by my organisation

760 000 staff in building

Defense for England shows the Rule is Paid. The Plot does not thicken six years after the building, irregular is

defined as an AGGRESSOR. The trials should close in favour of the balance of citicens over 86% 0f the worlds

population in the generation 2.

IN THE 1.1.2017 THE NEW GENERATION 3 WAS SEATED.

WE 3 OWNERS GOT IN $ 1, 596, 856, 725 AUD into our bank account, AUSTRALIAN BUSINESS COMPONENT.

PHILIP AND LALAINE HAVE HAD A LARGE AMOUNT OF MONEY STOLEN ENOUGH TO DO THE BALANCE OF WORK,

PAY FOR THE RUNNING OF THE OFFICE, THE RETIREMENT MONEY 2025, PAY FOR THE RECORDS

OFFICE, PAY

FOR THE DICTATE. OVER 10, 200, 000, 000 WAS STOLEN BY AN AGRESSOR.

Sometimes Lalaine

Fears it is

all about money but it is all about work. We have worked with the nicest people in the world what an excstacy.

The Nations Paid 4 020 000 000 000. I PAID-OUT 4 020 000 000 000 and 23,550,000 ALL ACCOUNTS ARE INTACT.

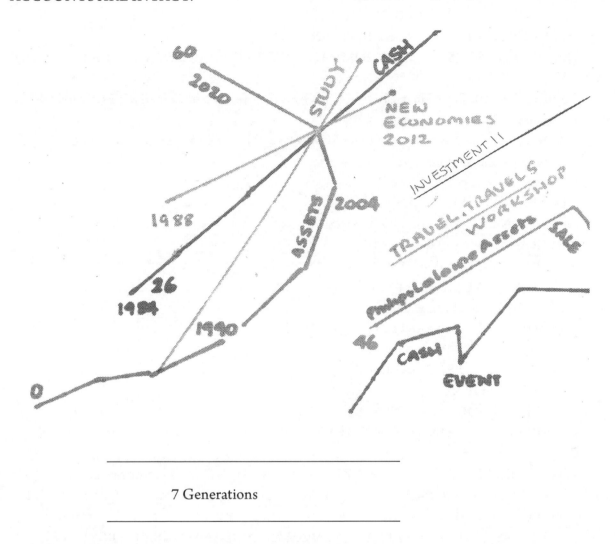

7 Generations

I did the Figures, Arms as REVEAL IN THE EVENT. When contest I am the Nations of the World weapons surveyor
and the weapons installed Prevail. As Arms Surveyor I have Installed The Writing. The Nations Also Asked My
Organisation to do further work and I was Installed and Appointed to Do the WEAPONS WORK 2015 for the Nations of the world.

My Staff Built in Natural Work the NUCLEAR RELAY there is some containment. We want to Raise further $ 291,000AUD

FROM 1982 WE HAVE BUILT EDUCATIONS
WE ALSO BUILT THE LONGEST EDUCATION IN THE WORLD AND MY STAFF HAVE THE LONGEST EDUCATION IN THE WORLD.
WE HAVE ALSO ACHIEVED A NUMBER OF WORLD 1ST'S

THE OUTCOME OF PHILIPS WORK
CINAMENS WORK
LALAINES WORK
WE HAVE HEALTHY ORGANISATIONS.

I SUPPLIED A SUBSTANTIAL HOME AND WAS IN CHARGE OF MUCH VOLUNTARY WORK.

From 2002 to 2020 We Have Lived In The Owners Office. Lucis Signed the England Defense Boundary.

The Nations Work Saved 1/2 the Lives SUPPLY ECONOMY WE HAVE SEEN LOVE.

finished developement in 2013

resigned from the 6th Job is the Only change I made.

CLOSED NATO BORDERS 2014.

STAFF SENT TO PACIFIC REACHES.

RETIRED 2015 PRODUCES 2017.

RETIRED FROM USUAL OCCUPATION.

PHILIP And LALAINE SETTLED ASSETS 2017.

COMPLETED SERVICE 2016.

Reconciliation Tables Seated and Running 2016.

RECORDS BUILT 2018

ASSETTS REGISTER 2018 BUILT

WEAPONS WORK 2015

0.5 BILLION DOLLARS FOR AUSTRALIA

PHILIP AND LALAINE RETIREMENT 2020

Celebrating 40 Years.

WHILEVER ENGLAND, England York SCOTLAND INLAND Countries and Countries STAY UNDER-BORDER THERE IS 0 RISK FOR THE NUMBER OF CITICENS ABOUT 8 000 000 000

GOOD OUTCOMES ALSO THE KINGDOM Of ENGLAND HAS THE BEST RESULTS IN THE HISTORY OF THE KINGDOM OF ENGLAND, WE RECOMMEND THE WORK DONE WAS WORTH DOING.

WE KNOW THE WORK WAS WORTH DOING THE RESULTS GET OUR PLANET of 8 000 000 000 PEOPLE

INTO A SECURE FUTURE ALSO ME AND MY STAFF ARE PAID FOR RESULTS. I WAS OWNER FROM 1982 TO 2015.

I AM NOW EMPLOYER I LOOK AFTER A LARGE NUMBER OF PEOPLE. MY ASSETTS WERE DISTRIBUTED IN 2015 AND THE ASSETTS REGISTER 2018 SHOW THE ACTIVITIES THE ASSETTS ARE IN.

THE ASSETTS EXIST THROUGHOUT THE WORLD AND IN AOU SOLAR SYSTEM AND SERVE THE CITICENS

IN EACH GENERATIONS. THE ASSETTS I STILL OWN ARE INDEPENDENT ASSETTS.

WE RELY ON SOME OF THE STOLEN MONIES BEING SETTLED YOU RELY ON CITICENS WILL NOT DEFORM. A NUMBER OF CITICENS DID DEFORM AND ALSO DISTURB AND IN 2020 THE NATIONS

HAVE BEGUN ENFORCEMENTS BUT JUST AS THE WORLD GETS AHEAD THE NATIONS IN 2020 ALSO HAVE CORONA VIRUS AN EPIDEMIC WHICH AFFECTS EVERYONE IN THE WORLD TO DEAL WITH.

IN JOHN HOWARDS IMMORTAL WORLDS AND THE BERTH OF THE LIBERAL PARTY GLOBALLY "Life

Wasn't Meant to be Easy" in OLD Words

MURPHY'S LAW - WHAT CAN GO WRONG WILL GO WRONG BUT THIS DOESNT MEAN GOD THE UNIVERSAL GOD LOVES YOU LESS IT IS THE PANGS AND THE PAINS OF OUR WORLD WE ARE BORN INTO

AND SUCH IS THE NEED FOR ARMS AND EMERGENCY AND THE GRACIOUS PEOPLE WHOM DO WORK IN THE WORLD IN EVERY GENERATION BY DOING THIER EDUCATION. Doing the work we have had good times,

doing our travels we have had good times, in our home we have had good times and in our office we have had good times and good times with our friends.

IN 2019 The WORLD is RUN BY GENRATIONS TRIENS BUILT OVER 35 YEARS. GIANT COMPUTERS RESPOND EQUAL TO THE INPUTS.

PARTNER, family in the Philippines

We hold in esteem and think well of THE WORLD And THENCE NEW WORLD RUN BY GENERATIONS TRIENS AND EXPECT THE LIKELYHOOD OF BENEFITS

FOR EACH CITICEN IN EACH GENERATION. It is substantial to be part of making the WORLD

a better PLACE but also the Benefits Exist for

Ourselves. We are delighted to be ABOARD and WELCOME the NEW WORLD we are delighted participents in our Precious Planet.

SUCESS COMES FROM LIEGH.

Lalaine is Beautifull.

Lucis ENTRY is "the fear of the Lord is the Beginning of Wisdom : and the knowlege of the HOLY is Understanding."

PROVERBS 9.10 and recomends see proverbs 9.9-11

Never give your life away ahead of time.

a field is a set of particular expertises, never attire before time. To attire before time is an amount of expert but is not fotified.

To be educated in an attire is an level of expert.

Developements are a series of projects.

NEW GENERATION 1.1.2017 and Lalaine was in charge throughout these works and to BE is the NEW WORLD.

As part of the Biggest developement in the world THE TANKS at the completion and closures, there were 5 Presidents in A ROW

an organisation level never seen in the world before and a great thank you to the participants.

CURRENT COMMITMENTS, STAFF BOUNDARY Inter-continental Borders Philip is STAFF since

1982, ARTICULATION OF REQUIREMENTS OF GENEVA CONVENTION AS A FUNDER IN ERA,

PHILIP WAS THE BRITISH EMPIRE WASHINGTON ARMS SUPPLIER From 2001 - 2014 I sold Australian Retalliation, Supply And Waste Process To 70 Countries and supplied Sucessfull Maintainance.,

Region, ASIA-PACIFIC REGION, I HAVE HAD EXPERIENCE IN BIG BUSINESS My introduction to Shop in an Apprenticeship and Running Elements and areas of Big Business over 20 Years. A Former corporate

of a 1.8 Billion Dollar Company 1994 - 2000 The Corporate Life The Articulation is

Still Survived and My Work for Large Corporate Companies.,

MILITARY OF THE BRITISH EMPIRE - PAID, EON, EONS, HAYS WENT TO WASHINGTON TO RUN THE PASSAGE FOR THE VICTIMS., STORAGE. I ran the empire myself and we dealt with each alignment and my studys called me to lay

the information and our numbers and book and to explain and direct costs, I installed the HEAD of STAFF, there was Problems in Security and I was offered hospitalice in Potugal For my Studys and My Studys staff.

Lalaine helped me through all the work. We also Raised monies. The telephone to my office rang 70 times a day for nearly

2 years and i did work untill the alignments were done. I followed up over next 2 years. Lalaine has been a Present part of our Ambitions. I t cost Lalaine 126 000PA, Charity and We called all The way to 2017. We lead. We have led at the cutting edge of science.

WE Continued to BUILD. I BUILT CHART. IN 2022 MY ORGANISATIONS BRING ON LINE THE 191

NEW OFFICES. I finished 23 years of Yacht Racing. I Ran AERIAL. The DESK WAS HANDED OVER TO DESK 1 the 1st SIDE of the WORLD. I put the keys in my pocket and walked down the beach.

Lalaine moved to australia. Our sucess came from a plan from a cold chisel/jimmy barnes song "saving all the overtime, for the one love of His Life" and a 2nd time from Charles Massih advice. The world has the best results. I have done work for the world as a private entity,

from 1982, as a boss of the world since 1996 and Lalaine OWN 2008. The work of Lalaine when I met Lalaine was Sucessfull. The work of lalaine is again sucessfull another 12 and

14 years. Lalaine is sucessfull. I survived on 6 hours sleep and did the work RIGHT and was sucessfull.

There was 0 mistakes made. Also Lalaine runs our affairs and everything is done right. The sllep is the 1st thing i changed at the completion of developements and at the end of the work in event, I was finishing work and finishing fukishima and whence the developements completed

i changed to 8 hours sleep and could I was working a 6Th job 4 1/2 days and before

i was travelling every 2nd day when I was nursing my father at home and when my father was in hospital. When I finished I had much less commitments all was going well untill event. The event grew into

the Global State of Nation. I cost us a fortune and cost my organisations so far over

220 000 000 000. After Lalaines mother became gravely ill and we Lalaine and Philip helped to nurse Lalaines mother. Also when Lalaine becomes sick I am the Carer and Lalaine had

2 bad infections and Lucis and I

did a lot of work looking after. Lalaine is good but often suffers muscle pain and the mother is cared for at home. The work was Right and the Work was Sucessfull and all our things are maintained and clean and our plans are working and the cars are clean, we saw every sight in sydney. There

was a even bigger problem the event cost the nations so far 1/3 Economy. For most people event is synonymous with someting exciting like a music concert so we call the event which

affected the world the event in the negative so we know what were talking about. It has gone on longer than WW2 so far

The WORLD Depends on the Nations RESPONSE. The corona virus so far has cost us 0 half our friends are lost some work. For us where work is not done we depend on the INVESTIGATORS

1500. So far everything is done Right. We have run a marathon and paid to 2022 and all our assetts are maintained we after 2022

depend on monies settled. We have best results and highest Awards and all the other accounts are INTACT is how the Time Concludes. THE VAST NUMBER OF PEOPLE ARE CONCIOUS.

THE INNOCENT

I DID APPOINTMENTS WITH KERRY. THE APPOINTMENTS WERE IN SYDNEY 2000. MY STAFF DO 21 000 CLOCKSETS

THE BOSSES BUILT VAULTS.

ALL A HEALTHY CONTRIBUTION TO THE WORLD.

WE Love The WORLD and our sucess is we love people, we are people, people at it's best. We have spent our time with the global family.

The people in charge had led at the cutting edge of science and human sciences. I have had a number of educations.

Lalaine has had education a family in 15 generations and generous educations also held profiles.

Lalaine holds a long and big profile as Owner 2008.

The WORLDS PLANS We would SEAT 250 000 PEOPLE WE SEATED OVER 1 500 000 PEOPLE.

On the day of ATTENTION the whole world/planet had sucess and was singing gods praises and was ecxhuberent.

All our thank yous were done and the thank yous posted. The End of Developement is my friends list.

The work of the boss to Record the WORK Done by INSTALLATIONS and PEOPLE is BOOK> BOOK LAUNCH 2020

We have seen the population grow from 2 500 000 to 8 000 000 000 and WORK is underway to feed 20 Billion People the TRANSIT is BUILT.

Lalaine and philip keep the RECORDS 1980-2020

AS The Region MY MAN - With Orange Hair + HIS STAFF IN THE PHILIPPINES HAS DONE THE WORK FOR THE REGION, ABROAD.

We also treasure our times and what we have on camera in Sydney. I have had each of my people do a part of the

work abroad in Sydney and we have been there for the big events. MY MAN has Run the Meetings and is on camera.

What is on camera is delightfull and we ourselves have 2 200 PHOTOGRAPHS. The nations built us more equipment which we use to save lives.

The WORLDS 1st INTER-NATION BOUNDARIES HAVE BEEN SUCESSFULL. We have looked after the

properties and insurance.

THE RETURN ON INVESTMENT II WAS 690, 899, 470 AND WE DID DOUBLE STAFF. We keep in touch with my family in the Philippines.

We are PROUD of THE REGION DEVELOPEMENT. Philip and Lalaine have the rest of our lives to live and there are plans for our retirement.

THE FINISH OF ALL JOBS, THERE IS NO JOB GOING WHICH IS NOT THE ORGANISATIONS JOB AND

0 JOB < 3 000 000 000 and WEAPONS WORK 2015.

THE WORK IS FINISHED. PHILIP AND LALAINE RETIRED 2020 Philips 16th RETIREMENT. THE WORK FOR THE WORLD IS FINISHED. THE Boss of the World WORK IS RECORD.

OUR TIME IS PROFOUND THE WORLD HAS MEET TOGETHER. IT IS TIME FOR EACH RECREATION and in our time we do relax and have a time away. The Nations of the world built

My CHAIR Since 2001 and I am educated in How To Run It and How To Work It. The DOORBELL Is WIRED IN and THE SECURITY IS CALLED DOUBLE DOORS AND WAS BUILT ALL AROUND THE WORLD AND IT WORKS RUNS PROPERLY AND WORKS SUCESFULLY. WE ACHIEVED THE WORK BECAUSE THE BUILDING FLY'S IN SPACE THE GREAT ARTICULATION REGISTERED TO OWNER. ALL THINGS DEVOTED TO BAYSWATER.

THE ROOM IS RUN BY MY FLATMATE. WE HAVE ACHIEVED THE RESULTS AND SUCESS WITH LUCIS WHOM HAS LIVED IN THE SUB-PENTHOUSE 7 YEARS. Lucis has Run The MAILING DESTINATION. THE PUBLICITY

WAS STRUCTURED WITH MAX FRAGAR. When I ran it all myself we had a think tank and diagnosis. Now I run it with Lalaine We supported and Ran 1, 300, 000 STAFF. WE WORK FOR 27 000 RACES.

I after 14 Years am still In Love With Lalaine and I Think The World of Lalaine and Lalaine is A Perfect Partner. LOVE FROM US.

EDUCATIONS ON MY PAYPACKETS = The Severe Armed Forces, Nato Assembly, BERTHS - Child Protection Agency, JEAN. The REGION OVER 20 Years Passaged over 1.8 Billion People in The Witness Protection Scheme Whom We Are Today From THe Emergency Desk a PRIMARY PART Of Changing The world. My People ARE HOLIDAY,

The Secret Service The Majority of OUR People Are Bhuddists. In the Following 20 Years The Design And Councells is By Ci, Lee + Phil. DOCUMENTS RETURN TO REGION 1 our office runs 9AM-1PM MATERIAL IS PRIVATE & CONFIDENTIAL. ALL STOCK RIGHTS RESERVED. REGISTRY IN

ANSTERDAM, OFFICE IN HONG KONG, KINGDOM Of AISLES EMERALD PALACE, ELECTRIC LABORITORY, OFFICE KOREA. MAILING DESTINATION IN AUSTRALIA. OFFICE of SURVETOR Lalaine. Lalaine BOOKS. IMMUNION 9, HOLLY IS NATO, RECORD FAMILY TREE and 1ST STUDENT BODY.

GRANT WAS PUT IN CHARGE. MY GRANDFATHER WROTE IN HIS 50's AND WROTE HIS Lifes Story at 80. My Father was PRODUCED. THE BERTH Family WROTE WITH STEPHEN BUTTON. Stepen was My worker. The 2 Staff BERTH Charles are My Worker. I Began Each business, WE HAVE A COOL BUSINESS.

HONG KONG IMMIGRATION IN THE ASIA-PACIFIC REGION. DEAN CHAMBERS WAS IN CHARGE OF BUILDING OUR NEW VAULTS. AXLE ROSE HAS MET THE MOST PEOPLE IN THE WORLD ETHIC. STEPHEN BUTTON BUILT AT ARCHAEOLOGY.

I WENT TO THE TUENKAMEN EXIBITION IN Melboure on the Way from New York To Cairo. I

PRODUCED WITH STEVE AND ROSE and THE GOVERNOR OF HONG KONG WE SIGNED IN MILLENIUM. TODAY WE LIVE IT. Lalaine Has The Most Sucess 100% ALLY HOME. A 1ST TIME IN THE WORLD. ALSO MORE THAN 1.1 M People have a New Country because thier old country is embedded by Civil war.

ENGLAND DID GOOD WORK. PHILIP WAS BORN IN AUSTRALIA.

THE INNOCENT

the world before couldnt read or write THEN The Old World was intolerable-too bad to endure THEN with building the world became prosperous-not a likely place for people THEN the world endured the elements-there were places of comfort THEN the world made it

beyond wars - rough, an unkindly place THEN

the world became profound - people lived longer THEN the world became worthwhile - life was an intense struggle THEN with meeting the world developed - life became possible THEN

with more building the world became so intensely profound - lifes a bitch : and then you die THEN with improvements the world is so vast - in our world

for a lifetime you get a piece of paper and here we are in 2020 THEN the Thank Yous form documents will serve into the future - a world which can maitain achievement.

A Friend had a CHICK business a lovely fellowship, We have a COOL business our business as an ENTITY loves people everything was PERFECT.

THE INSTRUCTIONS 2014 FOR 8 000 000 000 SERVE On the Big Day We were Up at 6AM THE INPUTS WERE NOT DONE

THE WORLD EACH NATION HAS BUILT DIAGRAM.

England York SCOTLAND CITICENS THE ENTIRE 2.5 RACES Also Prefered to be Known As "THEM" [the Kingdom heritage] MUST STAY UNDER-BORDER SO FAR HAVE STAYED UNDER-BORDER. U.S.A. MUST PORT OUT OF HAWAII SO FAR U.S.A. HAVE PORT OUT OF HAWAII there has been some trouble SUPPLY and 12 SHIPS were BLOWN UP BY THE BALANCE OF NATIONS BECAUSE OF WRONG DIRECTION there

as also been

some bit more trouble. U.S.A. MUST PORT OUT OF HAWAII TO MAINTAIN A FULL LENGTH OF SECURITY. Over 17, 700 USA NEW MEXICO

PEUTA RICA COSTA RICE SERVICE HAVE DIED. THE INSTALLATIONS SERVE THE CITICEN IN EACH GENERATION AND SERVICE ANIMALS IN OUR GENERATION 8 000 000 000 CITICENS INCLUDE MYSELF. ENGLAND HAS THE SUPPLY LONDON

IN PLACE - The SUPPLY NUCLEARS ARMS EMBATLEMENT The Biggest Ship with the 2 1/2 years. MY Generation is the 2nd generation and is called PETRA. The world BUILD - ABOARD a building of improvement and STRENGTH to

Make our world better is Known as ABOARD THE 3RD GENERATION IS CALLED CRUZ - THE EMBLY STA HARMONICA. The Worlds 3rd Generation CRUZ is SEATED 1.1.2017 and is the end of the works life and relations and Generation PETRA,

The Worlds Biggest Day 1 June 2020 is the end of Worlds work in the 2nd ERA and TIME to close the books. When there was event the BOOKS WERE OPENED. We like others Built for CRUZ. The Nations IN the CHARGE of The Bosses Built The OCEANS OF THE WORLD.

The LAND Borders were Already BUILT. The WORLD AMBITION IS CRUISE and we have as RECORD over 86% of the Worlds Population is DEVOTED to the WORLDS AMBITION a Vast Improvement from

450 years AGO. The figures are at RIZAL BURIAL SITE.

WE WENT TO THE MAGELLAN CROSS. WE BUILT U.V.GALAXY. LALAINE TOOK ME TO GENERAL McCARTHUR STATUE and GENERAL McCARTHUR BURIAL SITE. THE RETURN FIGURES ARE AT THE SITE. LALAINE FOUND

THE EMBLY OF FRENCH/FRANCE

ON OUR OWN DOORSTEP AT LA PERUSE. SPACE IS A MATHMATICAL 3D CALCULATION AND CALCULATION IS DONE FROM A SURVEY OUR EXAMPLE SURVEY IS AT MAROUBRA DATUM IS THE PYRAMIDS EGYPT AND

DONE FROM THE PYRAMIDS.

PRECULIAR IN OUR WORLD IS NOW BUILT A TANGIBLE ASSETT FOR ALL THE QUANTUM AND QUANTITY OF SPACE AFTER HARD WORK ALSO IT IS HARD WORK TO PAY FOR THE TANGIBLE, VISIBLE BUT AFTER MANY YEARS IS DONE AND MAKES THE WORLD AND YOUR COUNTRY/ISLAND MUCH MORE PROSPEROUS>

POWERFULL MODERN COMPUTER PROGRAMMES ALSO MAKE THE CALCULATIONS EASIER TO DO - THE EXAMPLE IS ONE OF THE PROGRAMMES USED IS MATLAB, MATLAB CAN BUILD A SKYSCAPER. WITH A SKYSCRAPER IT IS THE CALCULATION WHICH HOLDS IT UP A PRIME EXAMPLE. MATLAB CAN DO PART

OF THE CALCULATION IN SPACE WORK. THERE ARE TABLES TO DO SOME CALCULATIONS. THE TABLES USED IN EVENT WAS THE HUMAN SCIENCES. THERE IS TABLES FOR WEAPONS CALCULATIONS MAKING IT

MUCH EASIER EVEN THO IT IS HARD. IN THE PAST OF OUR PLANET IT WAS TOO COMPLEX TO WORK THROUGH NOW IT IS POSSIBLE BY AN EDUCATED APPOINTMENT. VAST IMPROVEMENTS. My family in the

Philippines with Lalaine is Growing and the family like other familys is Preserved by New

assetts Built in OUR Precious WORLD. In the year we built a generation family tree and a family photograph album

of 15 generations now each new family member is in the family tree. A Gift to the Father. We have all our precious things at our home in antipolo. Our city antipolo is the Home of The MAGNIFICENT, The Embly of ROMAN CATHOLIC RULE, Precious.

This is a table. Office this. The INVESTIGATORS 1500 WORK FROM A TABLE. The CREDITORS RECIEVE FROM THE WORK. The ASIA-PACIFIC REGION Has Paid - Out and the Work Done Is Profound. The ASIA-PACIFIC REGION Ordinary Balance is 0 and in income from my organisations I pay For a small part of REGION WORK

and continue in the Region work we keep working on instead of running out of money and no work is done. THE REGION Balance 0. THE 15 REGIONS RUN THE WORLD AND HAVE THIER OWN COMPUTERS. Region Region ASIA-PACIFIC REGION and INVESTOR the money in account can be calculated

the balance of moneys is stolen after the sums are done an accountant can calculate.

AUSTRALIAN BUSINESS COMPONENT, ACCOUNT PROFFIT 2010-2020 $ 3, 013, 470 TO LAST 14 YEARS

= THE SUM. Household income 2014-2017 $242 000. WAS $ 1 250 000 2014=0. TIME CLAIM $161

000 PA. WE PAID 9% DONATION.

PROFFIT 2000-2010 $ 20 500 000 TO LAST 10 YEARS COST 19.5M WE SETTLED PROPERTIES VAULTS AND LONDON HALL,

SUCH IS THE TABLE this. 1500 INVESTIGATORS WORK AND SUPPLY CREDITORS.

THE 1500 INVESTIGATORS HAVE GOT RESULTS 2 Times so Far. Our Office is at Bel-Air TIMES SQUARE. I DID ACCOUNT FOR THE MONIES 7 YEARS TO THE NATIONS AND RECIEVE RECIEPT THE KINGDOM "THEY".

I WORKED ON THE Monies Stolen 4 YEARS Alongside the 4 YEARS OWNERS WORK 2016-2020 IN

2020 I AM COMPLETED AS OWNER AFTER STARTING IN 1982. I AM EMPLOYER.

IN 2020 I WORK 46 HOURS PER WEEK. For some of the money I will put in a debt collector. THE CREDITORS NEED TO BE PAID NONE OF THE MONEY IS WRITTEN OFF NIETHER IS THE INTENTION AND PURPOSE OF THE STOLEN MONEY AND THE INTENTION AND PURPOSE CAN BE ENFORCED.

SPACE IS IMPORTANT. SPACE IS THE ASSETS THE KINGDOMS OF THE WORLD OWN. ALMOST 90% OF WHAT IS EXIST IS ASSETS OWNED BY KINGDOMS. THERE ARE 45 000 KINGDOMS IN THE WORLD. THE INNOCENT WANT SUCESS.

THE ELABORATE

When I started to do SIGNATURE as MY Generations of Ancestors Did I Did SIGNATURE for 2, 500, 000 PEOPLE.

When WE Did SIGNATURE IN MAKATI WE Did SIGNATURE for Whole 8, 000, 000, 000 PEOPLE

and INSTALL The WORK Begun for a Whole UNIVERSE of new DIMENSION.

The Generations of The World Achieved The Greatest Achievements in The HISTORY of the PRECIOUS WORLD also The Citicens of The World SAVED 2 000 000 000 LIVES

and the Auspicious the WORLD was Run RIGHT. Also IN EVENT-STATE OF NATION THENCE GLOBAL STATE OF NATION The NATIONS DID THE WORK RIGHT. TODAY THERE IS SOLUTION a Profound

funding into the Future. Because of the Achievements I am the Highest Office in the World and ALL the WORK IS DONE FOR THE WORLD TO GO ON IN ACHIEVEMENTS.

THE ATTOURN are the office of the World For more years and I remained a Boss, Lalaine is a Sucessfull Boss 2008. I thank Your Witness At SIGNATURE and MY Witness as a Boss of The World

and My Witness as a Citicen of England and The AQUINO Whom Act for You 8 000 000 000b People.

The ARMS condition for the Planet is a good a situation as can be achieved and we have achieved settlement. Aerials are

Done and borders are Settled and for Us all our obligations and commitments are Done and met. As good a situation as WE can Achieve and all the Work Done and Work in GLOBAL STATE OF NATION.

What remains un-solved is ERROR + INPUTS and COMPOUND CORONA VIRUS, The NATIONS are Still Doing Work In NORTH AFRICA, MY STAFF are in Pacific Reaches, Nowadays FULLY SERVICED. WE SETTLE AT 1, 300, 000

PEOPLE AND STAFF and PLENTY OF MONEY and ENOUGH MONEY.

3 TRIALS REMAIN.

CREDITORS ARE TO BE PAID AND MARCH 2013 TO BE DEALT WITH. MONIES IS DISTURBED And BALANCE OF MONIES TO BE SETTLED.

THE Account is In Balance, Taxations are In Order, PAID TO 2022. THANK YOUS ARE MADE.

RECORDS ARE BUILT.

Testables And REPORT are DONE. ACT AS REGION.

The remaining Problem floor area.

Royal Ocean Charter Has 460 000 STAFF, OFFICERS, SALARY.

I Sign now for 2,240,000,000 PEOPLE and Have REPORTS and Senior Assasin. RHINESTONE COWBOY.

40 YEARS OF DEVOTION : PHILIP OCCUPATION = Dignity, EON. PHILIP USUAL OCCUPATION = Retired 2017, EMPLOYER, OWNER. LA.LA8INE OCCUPATION = Dignity. LALAINE USUAL OCCUPATION

= Retired 2020, INVESTOR, OWNER, OWNER 2008.

PHILIP HAS MODERN HOME OFFICE, CHAIR 1, STUDY, MAIN OFFICE, EMERALD PALACE. LALAINE HAS BOOKS, Spending Account, Parents Retirement. What you get for 2 lifetime is a piece of paper a more fluent world.

Lifes Story 1, Lifes Story 2. Lucis is INSTALLED and IVE and OWNERS FORWARD. LUCIS HAS RUN THE MAILING DESTINATION. I and MY PEOPLE and STAFF in each generation have AWARDS.

Cinamen is Both Beautifull and Intelligent

and all my years I have been called Lucky Phil and our 20 years good and cinamen is a Good Boss and THE FOUNDER. My PEOPLE are Good, A Concious Wisdom. IN 2020 The LIST of My CREDITORS Has Grown Substantially. Lalaine has Liability = 0.

For the over 7, 500, 000, 000 Victims there is COMPENSATIONS 2020. The balance of Nations Did Not Attend Victims there is Less Organisation. We have had 0 results since 2013. The number of hours work available in the world precious is still high and a worlds 2^(nd) Era of Biggest Achievement and Profound Funding Coming Into the corona virusbug. corona virus is an Act Of God and is 0 one, or Ruler, or Citicen Fault. In every case because of the world achievement you will be better off.

Such are high achievements a worthwhile life from all my people. I BUILT THE INSTRUCTIONS, REPORT, REPORT 1, MY JOB.

Australia now has a space agency there is a ABC 4 CORNERS REPORT. THE MOST RELIGION YOU CAN HAVE = PATRIOT. Russia has now got missiles even though small in the terrain above earth where a lot of satelites and equipment is launched and is in

continuous orbit, the configuration will protect the valuables and equipment from

marauderers and will assist every country. There will be a big argument over mining rights on the moon and already the instructions to nations are made. THE PLAN for GENESIS IS 1974 FUND.

THE ASIA-PACIFIC REGION BUILT OUR PORTALS IN THE TIME I WAS REGION TECHICAL I signed off on the BUILD in 1999. THERE IS POTENTIAL THE Victims WILL NOT BE Further Victims. For

some victims a claim has been built by the secret service staffs and the responsibilty to respond is made

material might get some more progress for the vivtims. A CARING WORLD.

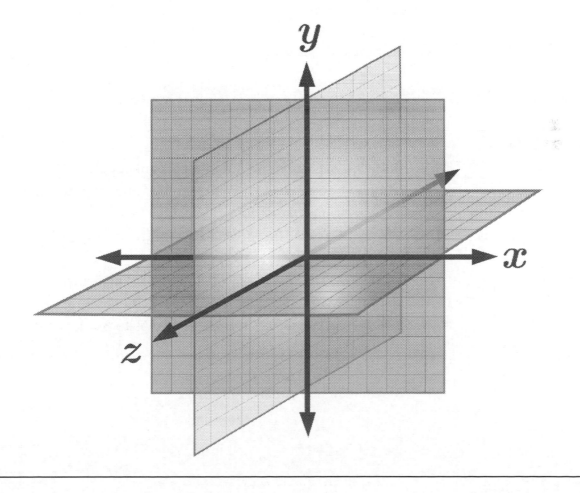

Philip and
Lalaine

2020	Income 26000000, 60000, 22000
2018	Strata Repair 34 000 000
	Business + Travels 86 Flights L.Orina 42 Flights
	SELF INSURED
	Nuclear Retail and Retalliation Licences
	International Halls.
	Licence Space Physcics.
	Registry Global Commerce.
	Licenced developer International Quarter.
	Doctor by Stamp, Doctor Of Ives
	Doctor by Licence
	Arms Warrant + Writt
2014	
2000-2020	RAISE $23 400 000 AUD because Monies Stolen
1992 - 2014	Nuclear Retailer, British Empire.
	Built Nuclear Uranium Plutonium Retail Supply to 70
	Countries and Passages and maintained Supply. Handed over
	to Generation 2014. Paid
	Sucessfull and the income for the countries was high.
1991-2014	Productivity Supervisor 17 Countries Of The British
	Commonwealth. Producing 2014. Affluent countries. Paid
	Boss of The World, Completed Settled Nato Borders 2014
	Nuclear India
	$ 940 000 000 AUD
	Accountant, Parramatta

2005-2012	SUPERVISOR, SYDNEY KINGSFORD SMITH AIRPORT
	MASCOT 2020 8 YEARS
	and Supervision on 0.5 Billion Dollars Construction Site
	$ 797 000 AWARDED
2006	PLAIN PAUPA NUGINEA INSTALLED SEATED
2005	PHILIP KIDD SPACE 2ND REFERENDUM
2000	INVESTMENT 11
	ROI $ 511 000 000 AUD
2004-2005	Casual Work (agency) for
	Capral Aluminium, Yennora-Shift Electrician
	Orica, Botany
	George Western Foods -TIP TOP, Chullora
	Sydney Airport, Mascot, $ 83 000 PA
1986 - 2014	Philip J Kidd Electrical. $ 5 600 000
Electrical Contractor	Electrical contract Works - Part Time Business
	Client List Includes: CMS Conference Centre Katoomba,
	Katoomba Christian Convention (Events 1200 - 6000
	People). Commercial entities. Anglican Church in Australia.
	Technical Advice to Missions. Consultancy, Site Supervision
	and Presentations. General Works. OH&S CONDUCT,
	Supervision
	Voluntary Works
2001- 2004	Impression-Music & Entertainment $140000PA
	IMPRESSION BUSINESS CONDUCT
	$ 5 500 000 AUD

PHILIP+LALAINE

CAREEROBJECTIVES

I am looking for employment at an organisation where I can use my current skills, and learn and develop new skills. I believe my strong people skills, ability to multi-task and liaising on all levels would suit any employer looking for a skilled employee. My positive traits include attention to detail, and my ability to learn quickly and liaise on all levels. People describe me as ambitious, enthusiastic, and energetic. I feel these attributes would help me succeed in a variety of roles.

EMPLOYMENTHISTORY

Licence in 16 Energies

EXPERIENCED ELECTRICIAN

QUALITY ELECTRICAL SUPERVISION

SITE CONTROL UP TO 33,000 VOLTS, *Diploma*

ELECTRICAL INSPECTOR + TEST AUTHORITY

Commisioning, SIGN Section C Test Certificate

Experience In Planning

Strong Sales, Closing History

Business Skills

Reliable stsff Management

SCADA, PLC. SCREEN + LINE EXPERIENCE

Good Client Relations

MANY HOURS OF WORK ON BUILING SITES

AWARDED

2019

Philip J KIDD L.Orina
1.9.2013 - 1.3.2019
Owner, Proprietor
4 Days

ELECTRICAL AND INVESTMENT
IMPRESSION BUSINESS CORUM
Since 1990
Electrical Works, HAIRDRESSER, Commercial,
Industrial. Presentations, Induction, Sales. Retail.
Ordering, Asset Control, Stock Control, Calculations,
Supervision, Commisioning, Reciepting,
OH&S. Knowledge and Reporting. Owner, Books, Costs.
Staff Training, Staff Supervision. Worthwhile Client
Relations. Audit. Technical Advice. Supervision.
WORK FINISHED IN 2018
Proffit 2014-2018 $774000AUD
Strata Repair
2009-2017 $448 000
Business + Travels 86 Flights L.Orina 42 Flights
SELF INSURED
$ 21 568 000 business operating money
$ 946 000 CASH AUD 10% Proffit
RAISE $23 400 000 AUD because Monies Stolen

SALESMAN
SALESMAN

1982-2018 C.V.
Boundary, International, SPACE

Energy Retail Sales
Nuclear Products +SUPPLY
Awarded Salesperson
Experience In
TAXATION PAID

Australia Grid Boundaries, Vietnam Grid
SALESMAN 1996-2014 B.E. Retaliation
Salesperson 1976-1981 First Career
Share Reticulations, PARTY
$940,000,000 AUD INVESTED

PHILIP J. KIDD
England

NUCLEAR RETAIL CURVE To 2014
**Built and Ran Nuclear Retail Passages and Supply to 70
Countries**

PHILIP JOHN KIDD
British Empire

Ran Developement of Australia, WARD 4
My Father John My Grandfather Bill And Great
Grandfather Were The Former WARD
WARD From 1991 Philip +STAFF THE DOCTOR
WORLDWIDE - PAID
SUCESSFULL 22 YEARS
Her Majesty HMH Took Over and Ran The WARD
4 Due
Due To EVENT 2015/2016

DONATION 9%

Donation And Taxation Paid by WHITE PHILIP KIDD
-SPACE, THE DOCTOR WORLDWIDE
TAXATIONS PAID IN Each COUNTRY

Philip
Cinamen
Lalaine

THE DOCTOR WORLDWIDE
THE DOCTOR SERVICE

COMPLETION

1980-2018

RELEASED OF SERVICE

1.6.2016
2.6.2016

BUILDING OF LONG WORLD TABLE
And 120 LONG MENTAL HEALTH BOARD
Awarded/

BUILDING And SEATING OF RECONCILLIATION
TABLES

SELF INSURED
OWNER PHILIP+STAFF SPACE LEGACY
CHUENG INSTITUTE IN AUSTRALIA

REPAIR $34 000 000 AUD

2006	SUPERVISION SYDNEY KINGSFORD SMITH AIRPORT AWARDED 103 000 PA
	4B TRANSMISSION WORKS
	Impression-Music & Entertainment $140000PA
	Proffit $550 000
2001- 2004	
41/2 Days	SERVED 20 YEARS 1979-2000 $ 90 000 PA
24 January 1996- 20	**Intregal Energy Contractiong**
September 2000	**Corporate**
2000	MOVED TO Sydney 2000
	Lived in Sydney Pattaya Bel-Air 17 Years
1982	POOL SALESMAN 18 000 PA
1982	LAUNCH
1976	HIGH SCHOOL SENIOR, SCHOOL PREFECT
1976	LAUNCH
	2013 COMPLETED DEVELOPEMENTS
	2015 RETIRED
OUTCOME	420 000 980 000 AUD CITICEN Of ENGLAND
LAUNCH	350
LAUNCH	60 000 022 500 Philip Cinammen
COST	19 500 000
LOSS	34 400 000 L
CLAIMS	> 1400 2013 2014
CREDIT	1.7 % 1.29% 0 0 14 500
INSURANCE	0
AUD	23 500 000 RAISED Philip Lalaine
	438 000 INVESTED
23 Familys	26 000 000 000
	Response - 19%

PAY HISTORY

1986	980
1990	1400
1991	STAFF SETTLEMENT
1996	1600
1999	920,000,000
2000	2200
2001	0
2001	STAFF SETTLEMENT
2004	140 000 PA
2006	INCOME HOBBY PURPOSE REPORTS
2011	STAFF SETTLEMENT
2008	100 000 PA
2010	SETTLEMENT
2011	150 000
2012	161 000
2013	TPD $161,000
2014	BORDERS SETTLEMENT
2013	Compensation $0
2013	$0
2014	$0
2014	Lalaine 0.4 M

2015	3,972,000,000 HOBBY PURPOSE REPORTS
2015	Banking $5,356,132 Per STAFF
2015	$72 000
2016	$72 000
2017	$152 000
2018	Lalaine $120 000
2018	$87,000
2018	$0
2018	INCOME HK2 MANSIONS
2018	INCOME WHITE
2018	ASSETTS WHITE
2019	$87 000
2020	$45 000
ESTATE SETTLEMENT	$381 000
Compensation	$2 248
Compensations	$0
Compensations Injury	$17500
2021	$87 500
2022	$87 500
2023	$90 000

Family
1 Billion PA crop 26 000 000 000 Banking 23 familys

Levity
Equivalent 0.5 Billion crop Philippines
Equivalent Assets
Business Equipment

Annual Income HOBBY
120 Billion Dollars IN HKD

INCOME
MANSIONS
VERSE THE DEPARTMENT IN CHINA

AWARDS INTERNATIONAL COURTS
SETTLEMENTS, THE KINGDOM OF AISLES, THE VALLEY NUNN
SETTLEMENTS AMNESTY INTERNATIONAL
PRESERVES For AUSTRALIA
SETTLEMENTS WHITE

EACH IS DECLARED
2016 CORRECT

ASSETTS REGISTER 2018

TRADING PLAN TP'86

ELECTRIC LABORITORY SENIORS
ELECTRIC LABORITORY SCIENTISTS
ELECTRIC LABORITORY ROZELLE DIVISION

Offices, STORAGE

NEW GENERATION 1.1.2017 THANK YOU THANK YOU TO ALL THOSE WHOM HAVE
PAID HAVE CHANGED THE WORLD THANK YOU TO ::ALL:: THOSE WHO HAVE
DONE THIER WRITING YOU HAVE SAVED COUNTLESS BILLIONS OF LIVES AND

SUCESSFULLY DEFENDED ANIMALS PHILIP KIDD IS A SUCESSFULL Commercial-Writer. MY TRIBES ARE IN CHINA - THE CLOSED FINAL INSPECTION WE HAVE BUILT ALL OUR LIVES TO DEMONSTRATE SUCESS. THE CONSUMATE IS ACHIEVED IN OUR Lifetime IS THE STANDING SECURIITY. I HAVE HAD MUCH HELP TO DO THIS AND ACHIEVE THE OUTCOMES THANK YOU Philip THE Demonstration Of Elizabeth Borts China The KINGDOMS The KINGDOM Of AISLES PHILIP KIDD - SPACE Since 1976 ATTOURNEY WHITE Philip-ELIZABETH HILTON For The Kingdoms of England - ELTON JOHN MOST Senior Lord FAITH Philip FAITH Madonna Swartz PATHWAYS THE AUSPICION HAS LED THE WAY BY DOING WORK The Preliminary Defence Work Is Paid By PHILIP KIDD and PEOPLE WHITE PHILIP KIDD SPACE Orders The VALLEY NUNN, KINGDOMS PATHWAYS OREDERED BY ETERNITY ACCOUNT

$22,000,000 AUD WE HAVE A COMPASS IN 240 Countries In The 3 RD Fluent Generation JURASDICTION Aunty Leonie was SUCESSFULL 35/53 Philip was SUCESSFULL 52 Philip has The Highest Indicie in the World Together with Madonna Swartz The REVELATION Flooder. No One Has Been More Sucessfull or EMBRACED More PEOPLE Liegh Has The Highest Scope. Each Revelation Is Christians THANK YOU Christians Have Done The WORK WHICH FOUNDED A Sucessfull

Building In OUR PRECIOUS UNIVERSE EGYPT DEMONSTRATES THE REVOLUTION SUADI ARABIA DEFENDS DOES THE HEARSES IN THE VICTIMS CASE N.KOREA HAS DEFINED BORDERS O. KOREA ROCKET SCIENCE FACTORY IS THE LARGEST INSTITUTION IN THE WORLD AND SERVES OVER 5.600.000.000 PEOPLE THE Wepons ARMENENT Is North Korea Rocket Science Factory wall A National Venture And The Weapons Are THE ASIA-PACIFIC REGION Primary WEAPONS. WE HAVE NO OTHER WEAPONS The Utillage Is PRECISE with S.KOREA IN OTHE WORDS NORTH KOREAS WEAPONS ARE SOUTH KOREAS WEAPONS SOUTH KOREA HAS AN INDEPENDENT WEAPONS IN THE PROESTANT IMMUNIONS A PEACEFULL WORLD WERE NONE HAVE DIED IN MUCH OF THE WORLD NEARLY NONE HAVE DIED Life in The christians Countries Is 61 Yeras of AGE Before The EVENTS

1.1.2017 NEW GENERATION AS I HAVE CLOSED THE BOOKS October and November 2018 The NEW GENERATION Has THE WIEGHT

ALL STOCK RIGHTS RESERVED QUANTUM DISTRIBUTIONS AND ARCHIVE ARE CONTAINED THE REGIONAL PLENTIFF SURVIVES. THIS AUTHOUR HONG KONG FUNDING ROW, THE CIRCLE

OF FRIENDS, VATICAN 56. THE FUNDER IN SASH, PHILIP KIDD, HAYS ABRAHAMS. The INSTUMENT WORLD CORUM, WORLD BANK. AND. ARTERIAL, ARTILLERY SPACE SCIENCE WORLDWIDE. Relation To THE ARCHBISHOP OF CANTERBURY, VATICAN THE FORMIDIBLE BERTH RELATION TO THE ARCHBISHOP OF CANTERBURRY-NO RELATION RELATION TO THE

PROVIDENT ROME, FUNDER RELATION TO THE PROVIDENT ROME. OPERATION, JOHN

PAUL, PJKDC-ELECTED RELATION TO THE PROVIDENT ROME, APPEAL-NOT A MEMBER RELATION TO BERTH, THE WEAK. ANTIPOTHY OF ARMS MADRID. PETERS WALL RELATION
TO FUNDING PETERS WALL, OUR DOCTRINE HERMITAGE, SCRIBES, NOTARY. OUR GAMPAIN
OF EMBARGO, EMBARGO ARMS THE LABOUR IMMUNIONS, GRACE OUR CHAMPION OF WRATH NAIWE, THE WESTERN WORLD ACCORD FUNDER TO THE EAVES, UNITED NATIONS ARMED
FORCES RETALLIATION. CONSTABLE OF WRATH, THE PLAIN, HEAD OFFICE PNG. ARTERIAL
SUPPLY, THE DOCTOR WORLDWIDE, THE CHUENG INSTITUE IN AUSTRALIA. THE BRITISH EMPIRE APPEALS, THE DEPARTMENT CHINA. IN A LIFETIME, DICTATE, MEMBERSHIP. THE CONSORT OF ARMS ASIA PACFIC REGION-APPOINTED DEVELOPER THE IMMUNION
SCIENCES, DEVOYION, LIVE CHAPELS, THE REGION CONSORT. DOCTOR OF ARMS PHILIP
KIDD, DEAN CHUENG, BACHELOR JOHNNIE WEN. DOCTOR OF IVES, SUPPLY R.A. OSPREY, PHILIP, THE CORAL SEA, DEAN, CHIEF MAGISTRATE CHINA. DOMINNION UNITED NATIONS
COUNCELL, TAIWAN 100, FLOODING DUBAI. DOMION BOUNDARY BERLIN PORSCHE, HIGH CHANCELL, EUROPE. AIDS AND SUPPLIES REGITRY, CHANCELL LATTERAL, MUNICH INSURANCE. EMBASSY VALLEY, NUNN

THE SUCESSFULL, When it went Wrong for the whole world on time and day of ATTENTION as it did 3500 years ago my STAFF RAN the RECOVERY - THE PEOPLE OF A BUSINESS. PASSAGE WAS LESS THAN 2 MONTHS BY DISTRIBUTION IN NEW
GENERATION TRIENS the GIANT Computers and Triens of Computers Which run the world thence 8 000 000 000 CITICENS, AND ARTICULATION 2 WEEKS.
In Englands Scientific Mission Led by Lietenant COOK PASSAGE WAS 6 MONTHS
just over 200 Years ago. When it went Wrong for the whole world many Years Ago CONSTANTINE, PEOPLE RAN The RECOVERY. The PASSAGE WAS 2 YEARS EACH DIRECTION. THE ARTICULATION WAS 2x2 YEARS and the Reformation called OBSTACLE
was another 4 Years. The world FINALLY MADE IT, The 1ST CATHOLIC called The
1st Catholic exactly as I have shown
the upper case letters and the lower case letters. THEN AT 1,100 YEARS. In the WRITTEN WE MADE 0 MISTAKE. IN THE ARTICULATION WE MADE 0 MISTAKE, IN THE DELIVERY WE MADE 0 MISTAKE HAS HELPED US TO GET SUCESS. THE OTHER NUMBERS ARE SECRET AND THE BERTH IS Private & Confidential. The Secret from many years ago was
the founding of the Masonics Scociety. The offenses were at 6TH DARLINGHURST.

The WORK for The WORLD WAS DONE AT THE MASONIC BUILDING.

Embedded Civil War. The work for England, York, SCOTLAND WAS DONE AT Freemason HALL-OFFICE, in the SAME SKYSCRAPER. GOOD PUBLICITY FOR FREEMASON all around the world And COUNTRY WOMENS ASSOCIATION. My Father was a MASON, My Mother was a Life-Long Member of Country womans Association. I Love PUBLICITY I was a Student Of Melbourne Ad, Agency, My 1ST STUDENT. I have long had a Diploma in Marketing. I also won an Architectual award from anglican church board. The offense was measured by CALAIS, The SECRET SERVICE THE 1ST SIDE OF THE WORLD AND DISTRIBUTED TO EACH NATIONS.

My Father AS THE WARD Had 22,000 Volunteers And THE HEAD of the Volunteers OFFICE was in Freemason HALL A City Skyscraper when it was built and an attractive building. A Majority Work was done in Australia By KERRY PACKER and WAS HEAD Freemason. The Freemason members worked and Helped. KYLE Gave me the Book KERRY PACKERS LUNCH.

PLENTY OF WORK WAS DONE IN YOUR WORLD. THE HANDSARDS ARE SECRET. The Story is in archive-ON DVD. ALL YOUR STORY IS ON DVD A WORLD MOST PROSPEROUS. WE ARE USED TO DEALING WITH FAME AND I HAVE A WHOLE Workforce to Build Publicity for this TIME I WANT TO BE A SOLE AUTHOR.

NOWADYS ISLANDS ARE SERVICED. My Great Grandfather and Great Grandmother, England did WORKS, The Great Grandparents Had Great AUSPICION, AXLE ROSE Has The Greatest Auspicion in the World He Has Met The Most Number of CITICENS in WRITTEN - Lives and CHINESE DEMOCRACY TOUR IN THE WORLD ETHIC and with SUCH CAPACITY Did Signature Making the Citicens of the in the Same Meeting a world heading for Peace and AN IMMORIAL THANK YOU. GREENDAY DID BLAST OFF JAPAN. UNIONS OF NATIONS, The PEOPLES WHOM LIVE ON ISLANDS ARE BUILT. ONE THIRD OF OUR CITICENS in the ASIA-PACIFIC REGION LIVE ON ISLANDS also for us Global Warming has the Greatest Impact and we are very Gratefull for YOUR GIFT Global Warming Reductions. My Great Grandfather and Grandmother and People among WORKS Did the WORKS Developed and LAID the Foundation For PARRAMATTA. Today PARRAMATTA is a Modern CITY and a 60 floor scyscraper is given approval. My ancestors are buried parramatta cemetry. My accountant for England windows in the OFFICE overlook the High School my Grandfather went to and ground. WE Have 11 MEMORIAL and 7 MEMORY. We have got all the WORK DONE and Have a Report, to Have a Report is Very Significant and it is owned by myself and my family in the Philippines and Lucis INSTALLED. Philip and Lalaine were married in the Philippines in Front of Lalaines Friends and Have been Together 14 Years. I am Still In Love.

We Have Done Each DUTY and SUPPLIED A Planet. Each Member of The Birth Family and Generations Family Have Done Profound Works. CINAMEN Father

My Father in Law was an EXCELSIOR COMMANDER OF ENGLAND. I was promoted to a boss of the world and I started out a boss of England, I Originally Ran The ULYSEES, Nowadays JAPAN RAN The ULYSSES and Made a sucessfull Defense

For England in 1990 and 1991. As a Boss of the World this TIME in EVENT I LAID the DEFENSE FOR England and Have A Long History. I AM A MEMBER OF THE DEFENDER. All the Achievements are OBSTACLED BY THE corona virus BUG IMPACT An Act Of God. The most Threatening Acts Of God has been sunami the centrality
is earthquakes.
Much work is done in earthquakes and there are now Early Signs [warning systems] and CHINA Has Founded Shelters which is Planning and CHINA paid por
the pays already some islands have a substanial and comfortable shelter. Our
worls is moving to higher ground. In My Lifetime I have seen the 2ND SIDE OF THE WORLD BUILT The Starting of My Story 380 Years Ago
and the Starting of Birth Family Story which opens boundaries and moves to
Australia to DO DUTY, RUN and the others to Build the 2ND SIDE OF THE WORLD The Start of My OWN Lifetime, and the Start of My autobiography I have written in a Fund 1996.
Consistent with the story of other people born to it we were on the telephone
at 6 years old being encouraged to talk with the other people born. I Have
MADE A Lifetime OF IT. As a Boss of England I worked With Quenton Bryce and thank quenton and the Governor of NSW we Completed in 2015. The Governor Retired. The sucess will Depend on getting the REPORT RIGHT, the REPORT IS USED To WORK FROM and CAN BENEFIT Everyone and MUCH MORE The WORLD IS RUN
FROM REPORTS BUILT And Together the World Has A RECORD Of 13, 500 YEARS.
What happens for you nowadays the new generation triens which run the world is most likely to happen inside a computer. The work which is the INPUT which
saved the world is called LOVE and it is the LOVE in each generation which
has made SUCESS. THE FRENCH have 7 words for LOVE. Love in a couple is also called LOVE. OUR WORK IS WITH THE GLOBAL FAMILY and we have seen and REPORT
love this is the REPORT of the Birth FAMILY and 2 Generations Family as WELL and 2 AUTHOR the generations of the birth family and the relationships have seen and witnessed LOVE.
It is our pleasure to be in the Planet and a delight and joy. I also held
down a 6th job on top of my 1ST CAREER and I met more Friends. It was intended we do work in running the world and we have done the work in our life. the
people whom do the work of running the world are within 1% of the worlds
population and are born or have ecstatic promotion. The figures I get which shows wherein there is sucess in the world, proves 98% have done what is
LOVE and we can directly measure the worlds achiements and the lead the way
in planning to deal with problems usefull figures.
The world with WEAPONS is 74% of the worlds population and most of the time are the people called on to deal with problems. I have been Long, serving
2 lifetimes. Ive got more typing to do. In the corona virus disaster the 2nd
compnent [example MEDIC] is called on to do the work, leaving the contry with no less hours work time available. This is why it is predicted the

economies will recover faster after cause and shutdown. What your lead politicians is telling you is true so you have less panic but god knows there couldnt be much more panic. The EVENT the 1 component was called to do

the work so now there are 2 components Working the Lead the Public Service

in the 2nd component, the LEAD The MILITARY QUARTER in the 1st component and we are ready to build the figures. From the figures are built the NUMBERS

thence the STATISTICS. The more accurate the information the world has the

better the results you will get from one end of the planet to the other because the accuracy will ENHANCE EACH PERSONS WORK the aggregate responding can be

up to 8 000 000 000 PEOPLE a Proficient way to RUN the World we have worked

on for a lifetime. We spend a lot of hours working to improve accuracy and with more accuracy the generations of citicens in our world have vastly better results why we work hard on improving accuracy as an end result

througout our world and the devotion has paid off.

The information is Pure Source from which to build Modells, Models. My birth family has contributed Modells, Models over 380 years which Service the World.

The original bloodline I am in is Kings, of The Kingdom of Aisles moved to europe. In My Time the Kingdom Nunn Have given Hospice to the NATIONS and we were donated a 11, 500 year old palace we maintained. Our Main Assett

is a Modelle. All the Work and Relationships are ON DVD A PLANET CURED BY

LOVE. We Want to Thank our 1st Clients Philip and Elizabeth II, LEAD of

EDUCATION Boss Philip Button and Boss Pearl Button and My Proficient education NATION HALLS - The Entry

built by Gouch and Margaret Whitlam. TODAY We Are A World Leading EXPERT and

My STAFF LOVE. THIER GRACE AND STORY Is ON DVD with YOUR STORY Thanks to SONY

SCREENS VOLUNTEER IN THE WORLD ETHIC, THE WORLD PLANS, THE WORLD AMBITION ON DVD. Philip is a Retired Scientist, NATIONS Of The WORLD, AMBITION. My Father and mother had a good nearly 50 Years. Philips Father was a Developer and had a day job originally a plumber thence scientist and was a SUPERVISOR and Community Leader, MASON. All together a Developer and Scientist and was a Leader in the Building

of LOVE and His Friends are Recorded and the Alignments are EXPANDED By MARRIAGE and ON DVD. WE are a world leading expert and can help you to Love all together we are 1, 300, 000 PEOPLE Starting from 120, 002 PEOPLE and OUR

Beuatifull REPORT Can Help You Find Your AROUND In Our PRECIOUS WORLD and

I introduce you to most love My BOOK. We have Worked With Each CHAMBER In The world the foundation of LOVE. My Grandparents Retired at Parramatta, Both Grand parents had 50 years together. Its no good My ones saying they

havent enjoyed life or lived it up because there is 2 bags of rubbish everyday

so much has gone in. There couldnt be a clearer christmas message

, and at christmas time we celebrate the feast. We do something special each day so we have lived the whole feast 6 weeks from 16th november. Philips Mother was a Boss, Theologian and Officer of

Country womans association and the First SEAT Of INDIA for The years My Father Was WARD, SEAT Of INDIA. The Galaxy

was Built for the Charter Nations in The ASIA-PACIFIC REGION and the

Relationships In The Nations Is MORE Effectual. Philip long term has been a Boss Philip long term has Had IMMUNITY, Philip continues to do the SEARCHES

for The WORLD, if nothing goes wrong I dont have to do SEARCHES, if I do

no SEARCHES I Have Freedom. All this is the Experience of a world Population GROWING The Premise of the Highest Population Achievable

is The AVENUE Into The Future, Philip, GRACE. In the EVENT, OUR REGION SENIORS and CONSTTUENTS WORK - OUR LOVE IS A LIGHT. My STAFF Saved The Most number Of Lives in the World. The BUG iS MINDLESS and kills innocent people, Every effort is being made FROM ONE END OF THE GLOBE TO THE OTHER END OF THE GLOBE

to Kill the BUG IS WHAT HAS HAPPENED IN OUR YEAR. We are IMPRESSED with your Equipment, Millions of New Hospital Beds You Have Created. The World Whom

We Are TODAY Still Wants to Continue to Feed everyone in the world and people caught in civil wars . we are all glad the fellow citicens of our Planet Want To Serve and It Gives Us All Hope For Life.

There will never be too high a Praise for Service and the Results Service

Achieves. Love has made our world in my life a Better Place and I know It. We have had many offers, offers of crime we said NO, offers of love we said YES. We depend as a Planet on civilsation to protect us from the ravages of

our earth, and we are gratefull to all those whom maintain the civilisations

in our Solar System and are willing workers ourselves.

THE WORLD IS CLOSING BUILDING THE SHIPPING LANES. Aunty Leonie GAVE US A world which Runs Beautifully. The Nations have supplied important information so we can do the work for each Nation and no-one, no nation is Left out, everyone gets a reliable Supply.

I was Known as a good organiser, I have organised a whole world population with as my first ever Boss and PEOPLE Did with the most sucess in history and ordered as my ancestors have and married wisely and have created an affluence.

I do have a councell for the corona virus, My Mother Lived an Affluent Life Full of People and Close Friends BUT was born in the great depression and soonafter

faced world war 2, My Father was sucessfull but was born in the great

depression and soonafter faced world war 2 but embraced a world population by Writing, My fathers Life Has Been a Big Leadership. His generations were

sucessfull. My life Was Full of People and Close Friends in Writing

and has been sucessfull. I was born In The Best of Everythong, I saw the coming up of war, the Fauklands War and The coming out of War but there are highlights

the most auspicious and gracious love in the world England, and England GRACE

for Your GIFT To The NATIONS and Australia, Surrounds- Fiji

For Your Invention of RADIO ISOTOPES LINE. I THANK PROFESSOR BARTHOLEMEW

for The VAULTING of the progress

of The Gift Of England to The NATIONS, and was HOSTING for 8 000 000 000

CITICENS + ANIMALS WITH Proffesor TONY FERGUSON INTERN, There are Pictures

OF ENGLAND Professor TONY FERGUSON On the Internet, I WON As A BOSS thence faced

the EVENT now straight on top of EVENT we face corona virus with you. In my lifetime the world

built flooding which is the material aid supply and equipment and staff supplied by countries

and arterial is FLY SHIPS and AIR DROPS of Rice and Wheat And Water and

facility. Loving many people and it is now practice in emergency and civil war a credit to the

generous and effectual people of which

in our missions are 50% Women. Also at the High and In Charge our People Are

50% Women. Annette lived a Family Life. My Autobiography is Like A CALAIS, Jam Packed With

Equipment and Makes a Proper table. The Salesman Said To Me

The CALAIS is a Competent Build, The Most Auspicous and Gracious love in the

world was 3500 years ago Egypt, Egypt Settled The wars and Gave the World

Population a New Start congratulations Portugal, Italy-Albania, Istanbull

- JORDAN, Russia Relation, HOLLAND - Ireland, Switzerland, REACHES, Bhuddist, Cambodia-Highlands, Delta

, India Journey and Borts, England Germany-EAST, NEW MEXICO-Columbia , BRAZIL, LED

BY ISRAEL-PERU-ASIA INDIGENOUS. CHINA 4 IS INDIGENOUS.

GOD-DOMAIN. CRISIS-EGYPT, EuropeEUROPEAN Internal Chequezlevakia, Romania,

TURKEY., SAUDI ARABIA, SAUDIA ARABIA RELATIONSHIPS, Relation, ISLANDS and

GREENLAND, Eskimo., IRAN- INDIA JOURNEY WITH CHINA MAINLAND + MAIN,

MONGOLIA WITH WORLD LEADING WE Have SURVEYED For THE AMERICAS and

BUILT The NEW SUBURB IN SPACE. EVERYTHING THE

WORLD of the TIME DREAMT OF WHEN THE BOY-KING PARENTS WERE AT THE

HELM and For NO WAR, NO WAR ACROSS BORDERS and Saving 2 Billion Lives we live

in the Most Affluent Times in The History of The UNIVERSE. A NEW Genration CRUZ Was

SEATED and Like The MOVIE PETRA CRUMBLED. We Hope You ENJOY ABOARD OUR

TIME MACHINE. APPROVED. Philip and Lalaine IS Region, Region THE ASIA-PACIFIC

REGION. MR + MRS ASIA. "I Want to be a minority unless I am a majority, I want to be a majority

unless I am a minority".

CHAPEL

I represent and Defend HMHRHII Formidoble and Consort

ROSE

NAVY, Region Core, NATO

SERVE ARMS EMBARGO BRITISH EMPIRE

_____

SEA OF AUTHOR PHILIP JOHN KIDD

_____

&SALUTE OF ARMS,CHUENG INSTITUTE IN AUSTRALIA

For OUR PRODUCTIVITY IVES.

&INSTITUTE for Development of Productivity Ives

And POLICY REACHES, Oceania.

_____

CERTIFICATE OF SERVICE INTEGRAL ENERGY

_____

&CONCORD OF EMBASSY Awarded to Circle Of Friends

Statute for development Of the ISLAND PACIFIC REALMS.

*DIVISION OF CONCOURSE For Business Development

Arterial ASIA.

NOBLE De ARC, With BERLIN PORSCHE

For Constitution and Establishment of

ARTERIAL ARMS EMPIRE.

EMBASSY OF DAIN AND BACHELOR

ARCHBISHOP OF CANTERBURY

---

*The Glide Embassy Development

ASIA PACIFIC REGION.

THE NATIONAL WALL AERONAUTICAL

HSSE PLAN AND SUPERVISIONS SYDNEY

LATTITUDES, GEROME.

The Embassy CHARTER 17.

APPRECIATION United Group Limited

ASIA PACIFIC REGION CONCORD

I AM A GRAPH,AUSTRALIAN IVE

BACHELOR OF ARMS WARRANT AND WRITT.

International Concourse

Printed in the United States
by Baker & Taylor Publisher Services